PAUL BYERS

www.paulbyersonline.com

ISBN-13: 978-0-9886185-1-0

Cover illustration by Andy Wenner,
www.auroraartcompany.com
Cover and interior layout by Stanley J. Tremblay,
www.findtheaxis.com
Editing by Jenn Waterman, Modern Elektra Editing,
modernelektraediting.com
Author picture taken by Star Morris,
www.ratstarcreative.com

To Sam

CHAPTER ONE

The 88mm shell exploded just under the right wing, lifting the plane and nearly flipping it over on its side. The blast sent a shower of steel rain slashing through the plane. The right flap and aileron were completely ripped away, sending a jagged four foot fragment of the flap slicing through the tail section and jamming itself between the vertical stabilizer and the rudder, rendering the rudder practically useless.

A smaller section of the aileron dangled below the tattered wing, held in place by a twenty-foot piece of the control cable. It fluttered back and forth in the wind like a fishing lure trolling behind a boat.

Shrapnel shredded the number four engine, the one farthest out on the right wing, causing the propeller to instantly seize up as the crankcase and cylinder heads were destroyed. The inboard number three engine was also peppered by flying metal and began spewing thick black smoke. Oil began oozing out from under the lacerated engine cowling, covering the wing like blood. The *Red Light Lady* had been mortally wounded.

"What the hell?" Captain Mike Perry shouted as the big bomber hung at a precarious angle, one wing pointing up toward the heavens and the other down at the earth. Hanging at this angle, he was barely held in his seat by his safety harness, and his feet were dangling wildly in the air.

He had to fight the urge to grab the yoke for support, knowing that one wrong push or pull on the controls would send the aircraft spiraling completely out of control. Perry braced his left arm against the side of the cockpit and finally gained enough leverage to slide his legs under the instrument panel and onto the rudder pedals as he grabbed the yoke and pulled back on it the best he could.

"She's not responding!" Perry yelled to his copilot. "She won't roll back over. We're losing altitude fast and she's picking up too much speed. You're going to have to cut back the throttles; I can't reach them. And help me with the yoke!"

When the concussion of the flak flipped the *Red Light Lady* up on her side, the plane lost the lift from her wings and started plummeting; she was now slicing through the air instead of flying on it.

Gibbler, seated in the copilot's seat, was hanging by his right arm from the side of the cockpit. He reached over with his left hand and swatted at the throttles, then grabbed the yoke. Together, both men struggled to wrestle the 36,000 pound plane into submission.

When the wing rocked up, it threw Jerry Idleman hard to the left, slamming him into his fellow door gunner, Tony Ramos. Both men ended up in a briar patch of intercom wires, twisted oxygen tubes, and flailing limbs, the floor now the left side of the fuselage.

"Man, are you okay?" Idleman shouted to Ramos as he struggled to his knees. The left waist gunner lay slumped against the side of the fuselage, not moving or speaking, then suddenly flopped over like a bag of potatoes as the plane started into a dive.

As the plane began to plummet, Idleman jammed his foot onto one of the ribs of the airframe and with one hand grabbed the base of the gun mount for support. With the other hand he managed to grab his lifeless friend by the collar before he rolled forward.

When the 22 pound 88mm German anti-aircraft artillery shell exploded, hundreds of metal fragments tore through the plane, making no distinction between metal and flesh. Bombardier Second Lieutenant Eric Blocker was leaning over the controls of his Bendix .50 caliber machine gun chin turret when the round exploded. A piece of shrapnel sliced into the heel of his boot, going through the leather and cutting into his sock, but not touching his skin. Another piece shot through the fleshy part of his right thigh, making a clean entrance and exit. A third larger, jagged piece ripped into his right calf, severing the muscle and shattering his leg.

Tommy Svensen, the navigator, who was less than two feet away manning the left nose gun, was not touched at all by the blast. When the plane reared up, it sent Blocker tumbling into Svensen, smashing his head against the side of the plane.

The wing lifted so suddenly and with such force, that all reaction was instinctive. Tasker, who was standing in the top turret, grabbed the gun handles to steady himself, but as he clutched the handles, his fingers also wrapped around the triggers, firing the machine guns.

As the plane rolled, he sent out a continual stream of bullets from the twin .50s at a combined rate of nearly 1,600 rounds a minute. As if suspended in a nightmare, he watched as the tracers from his guns rolled up into the Daylight Dreamer, the bomber above them in the formation. At point-blank range, the damage done by the .50 caliber bullets was devastating.

The stream of bullets caught the bomber's right wing between the number three and number four engine and chewed into the length of the wing toward the center of the fuselage. When the slugs hit the right half of the twin bomb bay doors, they tore it away leaving it hanging by a single hinge, flailing back in forth in the wind. It hung there for a moment then broke free and cartwheeled down the length of the fuselage, slicing through the ball turret, completely destroying the machine gun and killing the gunner.

Tasker immediately released his grip on the triggers, but it was already too late. He watched in stunned horror as the left half of the bomb bay door was completely torn away and tumbled through the air. It slammed into the right wing of the plane directly behind the *Red Light Lady*. It struck the wing between the two engines with such force that the wing buckled and folded up on itself, instantly sending the ill-fated bomber spiraling downward.

**The *Red Light* ***Lady* started to vibrate as the air speed indicator crept up to 300mph. The Flying Fortress was not built for speed and if she continued to gain, she would tear herself apart.

"Pull!" Perry shouted. By now, the B-17 had dropped out of formation and had lost nearly 4,000 feet. Perry and Gibbler were hanging from their seatbelts as the nose of the plane was now pointing nearly straight down, making it even more difficult to pull back on the controls and level out. In a moment of desperation, Perry maneuvered his feet onto the instrument panel and pushed back, using his legs for leverage.

The plane was shaking herself apart now as the needle topped 325mph. The yoke was vibrating like a jackhammer as both men strained and struggled to level her out.

The plane was nearly vertical now and Idleman could no longer keep his grip on the gun mount and hold the dead weight of his friend. The strain was too much; his hand slipped, and both men fell.

Ramos bounced off the top of the belly gun protruding up from the floor; Idleman just missed it as he fell. Both men landed hard on the wall that led into the radio room. Idleman lay stunned as he slouched against the wall. Even with the loud drone of the engines, he could hear the creaking and groaning of the overstressed airframe; he knew that this was the end.

He did the only thing he could remember from Catholic school and crossed himself; then he grabbed hold of his friend and cradled him in his arms—at least they would die together.

Svensen woke to find himself lying in the Plexiglas nose of the plane. When he opened his eyes, he was staring straight down at the rapidly approaching earth. Startled, he scrambled to get up, but his hands slipped out from under him. His eyes widened as he looked down and saw a pool of blood gathered in the nosecone.

Slowly he lifted his hand and saw that it too was covered in blood. Looking up, he was horrified to see that the entire compartment was splattered with blood, looking more like a butcher's shop than the inside of a bomber. His friend was hanging upside down like a side of beef from the gun controls with his arms dangling lifelessly, the lower part of his right leg jutting out at a sickening angle.

Svensen started screaming.

The plane continued to shake and vibrate horribly. The *Red Light Lady* was in her death throes. Perry and Gibbler just looked at each other, realizing that they weren't going to make it. This was their nineteenth mission, four more than the normal life expectancy of just fifteen missions for a B-17 crew. They had been flying on borrowed time and now it looked like their time was up.

Suddenly, the nose of the plane came up an almost imperceptible amount. Both pilots felt it at once and suddenly the fatalism that had filled their faces a moment earlier was replaced with the slightest glimmer of hope. With new determination, both men continued to work the controls and were rewarded for their efforts as the view of the earth that had filled the windshield moments earlier was slowly replaced by a view of the horizon.

As the plane leveled out, the needle on the airspeed indicator slowly dropped and the shaking and vibration stopped. Perry took a deep breath, realizing for the first time that he had been holding it. "What have we got?" he asked as he inched the throttles forward and concentrated on the instruments.

"Number four is completely gone and number three is not far behind. There's a huge patch of oil covering the wing, the right aileron and flaps are gone, and the wing looks like a piece of Swiss cheese."

"Sorry I asked," Perry said with a quick glance at his copilot and a crooked, halfhearted smile.

"Number three is starting to overheat. Once she goes we're done for."

Perry nodded. "Okay. I'll nurse her as long as I can, put as many miles between us and the Fatherland before we have to bail." He flipped on the intercom. "Is everyone okay? All stations report."

Silence filled his headset.

"Jeff, go check on the rest of the crew please," Perry asked of his copilot. "And make sure they have their chutes on and are ready to go."

Gibbler nodded and got out of his seat. As he did, he turned and saw that Charlie Tasker was still standing in his turret. He tapped him on the leg and asked him if he was all right. When he didn't respond, he tapped him again and then bent over and looked up into the mount.

"Charlie, are you okay?"

Tasker didn't respond but Gibbler could see that his eyes were open and he was breathing; he also noticed an odd, blank stare on the turret gunner's face, but the fact that he was upright and breathing was good enough for him at the moment so he continued on. Stepping around Tasker, he opened the door to the bomb bay and peered in.

Normally it was dark in the bay, but it was well lit now, with light shining through the hundreds of holes left by the flak burst. He shuddered to think what would have happened had the bombs still been in there.

He took two steps on the narrow catwalk that led from the cockpit to the back of the plane when it suddenly gave way. The far end of the walk collapsed, slamming into the bomb bay doors with a loud crash. The fall sent Gibbler tumbling forward and he frantically clawed at the bomb racks, seeking a handhold. With the condition the doors were in, it wouldn't take much to spring them open. He expected to see the doors fly open at any moment and he would plummet 15,000 feet to the earth below with no parachute. He had no desire to see the earth from a bomb's point of view.

His hand landed on one of the empty racks and he pulled himself up, swinging his legs desperately to get a foothold. His foot caught an empty rack used to hold 500 pound bombs and he clung to the side of the bay like a spider on a wall. When the doors didn't fly open, he gently put his foot down, testing their strength. Anxiously he crawled the last few feet and with an audible sigh of relief, reached up and opened the door to the radio room.

He found Joe Thomas, the radio operator, still sitting in his chair but he was lying across the small table that held the radio, hands gripping its sides so firmly that his knuckles had turned white. Thomas looked up at Gibbler standing in the doorway.

"Are you all right?" Gibbler asked. Thomas just nodded his head.

"Are you going to let go of that table or what?"

"Are you and the skipper through flying this thing like it's a fighter?" he replied.

Gibbler just smiled. "Come on; help me check out the rest of the crew." Thomas slowly relaxed his grip and got up, following his copilot.

They opened the door to the rear compartment and found Ramos lying motionless on the floor with Idleman cradling his head in his arms.

"Is—is he..." Thomas started to say, but stopped short when Ramos moaned. Ramos opened his eyes, looked at Idleman, blinked several times, then closed them.

"I must have died and gone to hell, 'cause that ain't no angel's face I see."

"Yeah? You ain't no prize yourself," Idleman shot back. Just then Mark Mitchell crawled up and out of the ball turret. His face was drained of all color and he wore a look of sheer terror.

"Lieutenant, are we okay?" he stammered.

Gibbler shook his head. "It doesn't look good. Number four engine is out and number three doesn't look that far behind it. If it holds out and we don't get jumped by any fighters, we might make it, but stay out of your turret for now, and everyone put on your chutes. Joe, take care of things here and check on Billy in the back. I'm going up front to check on Eric and Tommy."

"Yes, sir."

Carefully Gibbler made his way back through the bomb bay and into the cockpit. Tasker was still a frozen statue but he ignored him and moved around him.

"How are the boys?" Perry asked, as Gibbler knelt down beside him

"Ramos is a little banged up but should be okay and everyone else seems to be fine. I didn't check on Billy, but I sent Thomas back to check on him."

"Okay, go up front and check on Svensen and Blocker."

The copilot nodded, then opened the small crawlway door between the two pilots' seats and dropped down into the rabbit hole that led to the front compartment. When he poked his head out the other side, he stopped dead in his tracks.

The floors, the walls, and even the Plexiglas nose were all smeared with blood. Blocker was unconscious on the floor with Svensen trying to put a tourniquet around Blocker's right leg.

"What happened?" Gibbler asked. "Are you okay?"

"Yeah, I'm fine, but Eric is in a bad way. He was hit by shrapnel and has lost a lot of blood. I don't think he'll make it back to England."

"Is there anything I can do?"

Svensen shook his head. "Not unless you went to medical school and didn't tell us about it."

Gibbler smiled weakly. "Just do the best you can," he said, then patted Svensen on the shoulder and headed back to the cockpit.

"How are Tommy and Eric?" Perry asked as Gibbler got back into his seat.

"Eric's not good. Tommy is looking after him but he's lost a lot of blood and his wounds look pretty bad. Tommy doesn't think he'll make the ride home."

Perry sighed. "Well the *Lady* isn't in any better shape than her crew. Number three is still running, but don't ask me how and the controls feel like mush but we're still in the air so I'm going to press our luck and see how far we can get.

"Eric doesn't have the luxury of time that we do so I'm going to drop him over the next town we see. We're already down to 14,000 feet so I'm going to go ahead and drop down to 8,000 and hopefully avoid any fighters. Can Blocker make it on his own after we drop him?"

Gibbler shook his head. "I don't think so, skipper; he's in really bad shape."

"Okay, get him ready to jump and I'll ask for volunteers to go with him. I'm not about to order anyone to jump into certain captivity."

Even though Gibbler knew what to expect when he returned to the front, the sight still shocked him. Svensen had already bandaged the bombardier's wounds the best he could but Gibbler still wondered how anyone could lose so much blood and still be alive.

"How's he doing?" Gibbler asked.

"No change, sir."

"Okay, the skipper wants to drop him in hopes the Germans will take care of him."

Svensen nodded and silently the two of them put on Blocker's parachute. Gibbler cinched down the last strap and was about to return to the cockpit when Svensen stopped him.

"There's no need, sir," Svensen said.

"No need for what?" Gibbler asked.

"I know how this works. Eric needs someone to jump with him 'cause he won't make it on his own so I know the captain has to ask for volunteers to jump with him. I'll go. I know him the best of any of us since I spent the most time cooped up with him in this cubbyhole.

"Besides, we made a pact to stay together no matter what after our first flight over the Atlantic when we thought we were going to have to bail. And remember how we're supposed to all meet in New York on the first New Year's Eve after the war is over? You know how Eric is; he'd forget his head if it weren't screwed on tight, so I've got to be with him to make sure he gets to New York."

Svensen paused for a moment as he struggled to keep his emotions in check. Embarrassed, he wiped away a tear then continued. "So go back up and tell the captain that I'll stay with him; just let me know when to jump. Here. Give this to him," Svensen said as he took a crumpled piece of paper out of his pocket. "It's as close to an exact position as I can give him. If he stays on this course and the *Lady* holds together, you all just might make it, but you have a long way to go to get home."

Gibbler took the piece of paper and put his arm around Svensen's shoulder. "You're a good man, Tommy," he said, then disappeared back to the cockpit before his emotions broke through.

"Tommy's going to jump with Eric," Gibbler said quietly as he handed Perry the coordinates and collapsed in his seat.

"Good, I kind of thought he would. We're coming up on a small village now and hopefully they'll be able to get him to a doctor, so you'd better go back down and help him get Eric out. Sorry."

Gibbler nodded and wearily got back up and made his way forward again. No words were spoken as he released the small access hatch on the left side of the plane, just under the cockpit. He grabbed Eric by the legs and Svensen picked him up around the chest and they carried him over and hung his legs out the hatch.

Gibbler looked at Svensen and all he could manage to say was, "Take care of yourself, my friend." Svensen nodded and together they dropped Blocker out the hatch. Svensen held onto the ripcord and Blocker's chute popped opened instantly. Immediately the navigator followed his friend so they would land together.

In that brief instant, Gibbler found himself alone. As a kid, with two brothers and three sisters, he craved times when he could be alone and even as an adult he preferred to be by himself. But right now he couldn't wait to get back up to the cockpit to be with someone.

"Oil pressure is dropping fast on number three," Perry said. "It won't last much longer. The *Lady* is getting harder and harder to control, so when the engine quits, we'll have only a few seconds before she goes into a spin. Go get the crew ready to bail. I tested the bail alarm a second ago and like most everything on this plane, it doesn't work either."

"Okay, skipper; they'll be ready. Any instructions for them? How far are we from the coast?"

Perry shook his head. "I don't know, I can't read Tommy's note… there's blood all over it."

The copilot nodded, then turned around and tapped Tasker's leg; he was still standing in his gun turret. When he didn't respond, Gibbler tapped him harder. "Charlie, you awake up there?"

"What? Yeah. I mean, yes, sir!"

"What's the matter with you?"

"Nothing, sir," he lied. He was still in shock over what he had done to the Daylight Dreamer. He knew it was an accident, but that didn't matter. It was an accident that he had caused. How could he live with that?

"Come on." Gibbler tugged at Tasker. "I need you back with the rest of the guys, we're gonna be jumping soon." Gibbler continued on toward the rear of the plane, again holding his breath as he inched his way through the bomb bay. They were close enough to the ground now that he could make out the shapes and colors of the fields and forests below through the hole in the doors. Reaching the other side, he stepped into the radio room and then into the center compartment where the crew was waiting.

"Where's Billy?" Gibbler asked, looking around and not seeing his tail gunner.

"We don't know, he's not here."

"What do you mean he's not here? You never found him?"

"No, sir. He must have bailed when we upended," Thomas replied.

"It's not like him to jump without checking in first," Idleman added.

"Well, we don't have time to worry about him now. It's not like he could hide anywhere and be left behind. Eric was hurt pretty bad so the skipper decided to send him down in hopes that the Germans will take care of him. He's lost a lot of blood and would never have made it home. Tommy jumped with him to take care of him until they're picked up."

The crew was visibly shaken with the news that Blocker was in such bad shape and that their two buddies were gone.

Gibbler continued. "The captain thinks that we're living on borrowed time with the number three engine, because when it goes, we go. I want everyone up in the radio room. I'll open the bay doors, and then give the signal and we'll all jump together."

"Sir!" Mitchell said, his face a mask of horror. "I looked everywhere and I can't find my chute. I think in the excitement of this being my first mission, I must have forgotten it back on my bunk."

Gibbler just hung his head and shook it slowly. "A parachute is the one thing that you don't forget."

"I have an extra one," Tasker said flatly.

Gibbler was a little surprised that he had an extra one and he also noticed that Tasker was still wearing that strange, distant look, but right now he didn't have time to worry about it.

"Okay, go get it. I'm going back up to the cockpit and then open the bay doors. You guys be ready to jump and stay together."

Tasker followed Gibbler back to the cockpit, grabbed his chute and headed back. As soon as Tasker was safely across the bomb bay catwalk, Gibbler pushed the button to open the doors. They wouldn't budge.

"We got a problem, Captain!" Gibbler shouted. "The bay doors are all shot to pieces and won't open."

When bailing out of a B-17, the closest exit for the pilot and copilot was through the bomb bay. It was close enough that if the plane started to lose control, they could jump out of their seats, take a few steps and dive out to safety. But now they would have to run the entire length of the plane, and go out the waist hatch or try to squirm their way down the tight passage to the navigator's position and go out the same hatch that Blocker and Svensen had used. Both were very risky if the plane started to spin or went into a dive.

"We got an even bigger problem," Perry countered. "Number three is really starting to heat up. We've only got a couple of minutes before it goes. Get everyone ready."

"Come on then," Gibbler said. "Let's all jump together while the plane is still flying straight and level."

"Negative," Perry said. "I'm going to fly her for as long as I can. Every mile I put between us and Germany gives you guys a better chance of escape. Now get everyone back there and I'll signal you when to go."

Gibbler looked at Perry for a moment, then got back into his copilot's seat.

"What are you doing?" Perry shouted.

"Once the engine goes the plane will get harder and harder to handle. With the two of us muscling them, we should be able to get another seven or eight miles out of her before she rolls over on her back. And besides, we might get lucky and make it to the door."

"Thanks, Jeff, but you're leaving with the others. That's an order!"

"If you stay, I stay. What are you going to do, have me court martialed?"

"I'm afraid you both are leaving," said a voice behind them.

They turned to see Charlie Tasker standing behind them with his .45 pointed at them.

"What are you doing, Charlie? Are you nuts?" Perry asked.

"Both of you get up and go to the back with the rest of the guys. I've heard every word you said. I can't fly this thing as good as either of you, but I can give you the time you need to get out safely." He waved the pistol, motioning them to move to the door. "Now move! You first, Lieutenant, then you, Captain. Don't make me use this. Please."

Both men looked at Tasker and could see the pain and desperation in his eyes, and they knew he meant it. Gibbler slowly got up and walked to the back while Tasker eased into the copilot's seat. He looked very uncomfortable there, but there was a hard determination in his eyes that made him stay.

"Why?" Perry asked.

Tasker almost started to cry, but kept his emotions in check. "When you get back to base, just tell them it was an accident, a horrible, horrible accident and that I'm sorry," he said softly, seeing the image of the tracers hitting the plane that was seared into his memory. He paused for a moment and then the hardness came back to his eyes. "Now move, Captain."

Just then there was a loud bang and a huge puff of black smoke popped out of the number three engine. The propeller slowed to a stop and a moment later, flames started spewing out from under the engine cowling. "That's it. Now go!" Tasker shouted. He put one hand on the yoke and still held the gun in the other. Perry got up and headed toward the back.

The right wing started to dip, throwing both men against the wall in the bomb bay. Gibbler reached out to steady himself and cut his hand on a jagged edge.

"Go! Go! Go!" Perry shouted to the crew, then reached back to help Gibbler. Tasker managed to right the plane for a moment and the two pilots made it to the back with the others.

"Where's Charlie?" Ramos asked.

"He's flying the plane," Perry answered. "Now go while he still has it level!"

"But he doesn't know how to fly. How is he going to get out?"

Perry and Gibbler looked at each other. They both knew that Tasker had no intentions of getting out. "Just go!" Perry shouted again. Thomas was at the right side door hatch. He looked back and got a nod from Perry and then he jumped. "Go, Ramos!" Ramos crossed himself and muttered some long forgotten prayer. He didn't know what it meant but at a time like this he thought anything would help. Idleman followed right behind him. Mitchell stood petrified, looking out the door. "Go!" Perry shouted again.

"I-I can't."

The wing started to dip again and Perry felt the nose beginning to drop. He knew Tasker was about to lose control. When the wing dipped, Mitchell stumbled a little. At that, Perry put his hand on Mitchell's head, pushed it down and shoved him out the door. "Come on, Jeff, you're next. You know: Captain, last man out, that sort of thing."

By now the plane had angled steeply. Gibbler nodded, took a step, then dove out the window. Perry took a quick last look around, then jumped.

CHAPTER TWO

Ten minutes earlier...

"Okay, everyone, I want a gun check. Top turret?"

"Yes, sir," Charlie Tasker said as he climbed into his gun mount just behind the cockpit. Charlie was a third generation farmer from Greenfield, Iowa, a small town about fifty miles southwest of Des Moines. He was short and stocky with muscular arms and thick, wavy red hair. His father wanted him to stay and help on the farm, saying it was just as important to raise food for the troops as it was to fight, but Charlie didn't see it that way. He finished out the last harvest in the summer, then at nineteen went off to war.

He spun the turret in a complete circle to check the motors, then cocked the twin .50 caliber machine guns. A light squeeze on the trigger sent several shells arcing into open sky. "Top turret check."

"Waist gunners?"

Jerry Idleman and Tony Ramos were the waist gunners on the *Red Light Lady*, a B-17 heavy bomber. Carrying twelve .50 caliber machine guns, 6,000 rounds of ammunition and a 10,000 pound bomb load, the big four-engine bomber had lived up to its nickname of the Flying Fortress.

Like many other planes in her squadron, the *Red light Lady* was adorned with nose art in the form of a scantily clad beauty. The artwork was done by Ramos, who bragged that the inspiration for the picture came from his girlfriend back home. Everyone just laughed because they couldn't believe that a girl that good looking would go for a guy like him.

The *Lady* really got her name from what happened when the crew was flying across the Atlantic on the way to England. Halfway into the flight, the red warning light on the fuel gauges came on. Thinking they were running out of fuel, they frantically scrambled, preparing to ditch in the middle of the icy Atlantic. After flying for more than an hour with the red light still on, they relaxed a little and eventually landed safely.

Ramos was a twenty-year-old street kid from Los Angeles. He was a little on the short side but his cocky mouth and attitude made up for his stature. He was always in minor trouble with the law before the war, and when the last judge to see him gave him the choice of doing hard time or joining the military, he chose the Army. He would never admit it to anyone but he was really getting used to army life and was considering staying in after the war.

Jerry Idleman was a big kid from Middlesboro, Kentucky, a small town just north of the Tennessee border near the Cumberland Gap. He finished high school and one month after graduation, he and three buddies joined up together. They chose the Army because the recruiter promised to keep the four of them together. He had lied. Two of his buddies were in Italy and the third was dead, killed in north Africa.

Both gunners pulled back the receivers and test fired their weapons.

"Right waist check."

"Left waist check."

Billy Jacobs was a country boy from near Shreveport, Louisiana, who had just fallen off the turnip truck but landed on his feet. He was naïve, yet had a strange country wisdom that was hard to explain. He took aim at the B-17 following them, pretending it was a German twin engine ME 110 fighter bomber. He made a few rat-tat-tat sounds then pointed the guns down and safely fired. "Tail gunner check," he said, with a slight southern twang.

"Ball turret?"

After a few moments of silence, the captain spoke again.

"What's going on down there, Ball Turret?" Captain Mike Perry asked. The *Red Light Lady*'s skipper was a reservist who had worked for the railroad in the Minneapolis-St. Paul area. Perry had short black hair, brown eyes, 175 pounds hanging comfortably on his 5'10" frame. At twenty-six, he was the "old man" of the crew and the only one who was married with a family back home.

"Sorry, sir." Mark Mitchell obligingly test fired his twin .50s, tracking and shooting at an unseen enemy below. Mitchell was from Columbus, Ohio, and topped out at 5'4 and weighed 135 pounds soaking wet. His short, curly blond hair and face covered with freckles made him look five years younger than nineteen.

He was the ball turret gunner, not so much by choice, but by being born to it, literally. The turret was one of the most important positions on the B-17, being the only gun that could protect the underside of the airplane as well as one of the most dangerous. The turret was a Plexiglas ball barely three feet in diameter. The gunner had to contort his body through a hatch, then sit with his knees almost touching his chest. The triggers were mounted between his legs and the recoil of the guns was only inches from his face.

Suspended beneath the aircraft, the turrets only armor was in the hatch and underneath the gunner. Mitchell was also the newest member of the crew.

"Excuse me, sir," Mitchell called out from the ball turret, "I thought the S2 weather officer said this morning we were going to have clear weather all the way to the target and back."

"That's right, Mitchell, he did," Perry replied.

"Yes, sir, then how could he miss that weather front ahead of us? I've never seen such a black storm cloud in all my life."

Perry looked over at Gibbler and smiled and just shook his head. Before Perry could answer, Ramos got on the intercom.

"I got this one, skipper." Ramos smiled at Idleman, then walked over to the top of the ball turret and rapped on it a few times with his knuckle. "Okay, kid, listen up. The weather over here in Europe is a lot different than it is back home in the States. Here they have storm fronts that come out of nowhere and usually last for just a few minutes and then disappear, but their effects are deadly nonetheless, and they have a special two dollar name for these storms, they're called Fliegerabwehrkanone. In other words—FLAK!"

Everyone started laughing. "Ha ha, very funny," Mitchell said.

"Have you ever been duck hunting?" Ramos continued.

"Sure have," Mitchell replied. "Me and Pa went hunting all the time. In fact, one of the reasons that they made me a gunner is the way I can track and shoot a moving target."

"Good, then when you were hunting, did you ever have a really large flock of ducks fly over you? A flock so large you couldn't pick out a single target because there were just too many of them?"

Mitchell nodded inside the turret. "Sure did. One Sunday morning, me and Pa went hunting instead of going to church, and boy was Mom mad at us for that..."

"Okay, okay," Ramos interrupted. "How did you take aim?"

"Well, I just pointed the gun in the middle of the flock and started pulling the trigger."

"This ain't no Sunday morning bird hunt, boy. That's the Germans down there and instead of using shotguns, they're using 88 millimeter cannons, and instead of shooting at ducks, they're shooting at us!"

Ramos looked up and over at Idleman and snickered then turned stoned face again as he looked back down at Mitchell. "Do you know about the German 88s, kid?" he continued without giving Mitchell a chance to answer. "Best damn gun the Germans got. I figure there are about a hundred of them down there and each 88 can throw up a 20 pound shell, and most can shoot higher than we can fly. And a good gun crew can send up 15 to 20 rounds a minute without breaking a sweat."

'That's enough, Ramos," Perry interrupted. "You're scaring the kid."

"Heck," Gibbler said. "He's scaring me."

"Yeah, lighten up," Jacobs added from the tail section.

Ramos just shrugged his shoulders. "I just wanted the kid to know what he's getting into, that's all." He stifled a smile as he looked at Idleman, who was wearing his own grin at the expense of their newest crewmember.

"Pilot to navigator, are we on course?"

"Yes, sir. We should be at the IP in a few minutes," Second Lieutenant Tommy Svensen called out from the navigator's station in the nose of the plane. Svensen was a big blond kid from a small Minnesota town called Grand Falls, near the Canadian border. His well-defined Nordic features made it easy to see that he was a descended from Viking warriors, but the only plundering and pillaging he did was on the football field as an all-state linebacker. He had a good freshman year at college and even at this early stage of his career there was talk of his making it in the pros. But he wanted to fight for his country and not just on the gridiron so he put his dreams on hold and joined the Army.

"Roger that, stay sharp everyone," Perry continued. "I heard Tony bragging earlier that he's got a date with a cute little brunette he met at the USO last week in London. I wouldn't want him to miss it." A few wolf whistles and catcalls echoed through the intercom, but were interrupted by a call from the navigator.

"Okay, we're starting our IP now," Svensen announced.

Silence now filled the plane except for the steady drone of the four 1,200 horsepower Wright Cyclone radial engines. Each crewman was now in his own world, with its own duties and responsibilities, preparing for combat.

"I've got the plane," Eric Blocker announced. The young bombardier from Silver City, New Mexico, was peering down through his Norden bombsite, ignoring the puffs of black smoke that were beginning to appear.

The *Red Light Lady* was entering the storm cloud...

CHAPTER THREE

Billy Jacobs was kneeling at his tail gun position, keeping a watchful eye out for enemy fighters, although he really didn't expect to see any. The German pilots were smart enough not to chase the bomber formation into the flak. Jacobs had seen flak before, and plenty of it, but this was the worst yet.

When he first arrived in England, he'd heard the "old timers," those with ten missions or more under their belts, talk about flak that was thick enough to walk on. He'd always thought they were kidding, trying to scare the newbies; that was until his fifth mission when they lost nine planes from their flight, three planes from their own squadron alone to flak. That day had been bad, but today was worse. Much worse.

The *Red Light Lady* was the number three plane in the lead squadron and from his position Jacobs could see the entire formation. It was a large raid today with nearly 700 bombers and fighter escorts that stretched for miles. The smoke from the exploding flak shells was so thick it was impossible to see the planes bringing up the rear.

The Germans were beginning to get the range now and the shells were exploding closer and closer to the formation. Jacobs was watching the planes in the squadron, to his right and below him, when a shell hit the bomber in the center slot. It came up between the two engines on the right wing and left a huge gaping hole. The great plane shuddered like a prizefighter taking a blow to the chin, but she shook it off and continued on in formation.

The shell must have been set on a timer because it didn't explode when it hit the wing but continued upward and exploded directly in front of a bomber that was 200 feet higher. It detonated less than thirty feet in front of the plane, hurtling hundreds of pieces of shrapnel into the plane, shattering all the Plexiglas in the nose and cockpit, instantly killing the pilots, navigator and bombardier.

Jacobs watched as the plane immediately went into a dive. He saw four little specks emerge from the damaged plane that turned into parachutes, joining the 23 others that he had already counted floating across the sky. It reminded him of being back home in a summertime field with the air filled with blowing dandelion seeds.

Suddenly the *Red Light Lady* lurched sharply, and Billy banged his head hard against the ceiling. Dazed, he felt himself falling backwards in the crawl tube that led to the front of the plane. As he was tumbling, the chest strap on his parachute snagged the handle of the emergency escape hatch. Instinctively he reached out and caught the handle with one hand and grabbed the bulkhead frame with the other. The plane was pointing almost straight down now and he was hanging there like a swinging bag of laundry.

Panic swept through him as he looked down the long shaft toward the front of the plane. He saw the ammo boxes from the waist guns fall off the walls and scatter hundreds of rounds across the fuselage. He also saw Ramos and Idleman lying motionless in a heap wedged between the floor and the wall leading into the radio room.

Frantically he tried to call for help over the intercom but quickly saw that his cord had been ripped from its connection. Had he been knocked out and missed the bailout alarm? Anger now began to overwhelm the panic gripping him. Did they already jump and leave him there to go down with the plane? How could they do that to him? Were Ramos and Idleman dead? Was he alone?

Jacobs steadied his feet against the ribs of the fuselage and could feel the heavy vibrations running through it; he knew the plane was tearing herself apart. Quickly he reached up and twisted the hatch handle to untangle his chute strap. As he turned the handle, the door popped and was immediately grabbed by the wind and ripped open. Not seeing anyone else in the plane, and with it diving at a steep angle, he decided it was time to leave.

Jacobs grabbed the sides of the hatch and hoisted himself through. As he stuck his head through the hatch, the powerful force of the wind ripped his off leather helmet and one of his gloves. He pushed himself the rest of the way out and leaned over and slid down the side of the plane, past the horizontal stabilizers and off the tail until he simply fell into the sky. How odd, he thought as he slid past his gun position. He was now on the outside looking in.

Plummeting through the sky, he waited as long as possible before opening his chute, remembering stories he'd heard of some Nazi pilots shooting fliers while they swayed helplessly in their chutes. With the ground coming up fast and seeing no enemy fighters, he pulled the ripcord.

With a sudden and powerful jerk, his chute filled with air and he seemed to be suspended in time. Immediately he was struck at how quiet it was. He was accustomed to the loud, steady drone of four engines and until now never knew how much they had comforted him. His world was not completely silent, but everything now seemed to have a dull hush about it.

He could see the small puffs of flak as they exploded, then moments later hear their meager pops. Even the mighty roar of the 700 plane formation was quickly fading into the distance. He looked up in disbelief and watched as the *Lady* righted herself and kept on flying without him; suddenly he felt very, very alone.

Jacobs hung his head in despair and between his dangling feet saw that the ground was coming up fast. "Okay, farm boy, time to start using your old noodle," he whispered to himself as he started looking around. He was drifting down into a densely wooded area with the nearest village about five miles away. It reminded him of the forests he used to roam as a kid back home in Louisiana. If he didn't break a leg or ankle coming through the trees, he knew he would have a good chance of avoiding the Krauts.

He tugged on the shroud lines, doing his best to steer toward a small grassy meadow that was rising up fast to meet him. He slammed into the ground and tumbled over several times, tangling his legs in the lines. He sat up and began pulling at the lines like a cat playing with a ball of yarn, trying to untangle the lines from around his legs.

He quickly gathered up his chute and ran into the nearby trees. The natural reaction would be to run, but he realized that without knowing exactly where he was, he had just as much chance of running into the Germans as he did of running away from them. Quietly, he lay along the roots of an oak tree and just watched and waited.

CHAPTER FOUR

Lt. Tommy Svensen kept one eye on the *Red Light Lady* and the other on his friend Eric Blocker. Blocker hung motionless under his parachute while the image of the *Red Light Lady* quickly faded to just a tiny speck in the sky. Despair was his new companion as he hung suspended between the heavens and the earth, wondering what he should do now.

The flak had stopped and the air was still, but the ugly black patches of the exploded shells still hung in the sky, marking where a great battle had just taken place. Soon even that would be gone, cleared away by the wind, and he would be alone again. He tugged on the chute cords, trying to steer a little closer to his friend.

The scenery was beautiful, with rich green farmlands and grazing livestock. The wind caught his chute and spun him a little to the right and the scene quickly changed. Gone was the peaceful country setting, replaced by the cold reality of war.

There was a small river winding through the countryside with a village nestled on both sides of its banks. Scattered in the river were the remnants of an old stone bridge that had connected the two communities. But someone somewhere in high command decided that the bridge had some military significance and had it bombed. Suddenly he felt very sad.

Blocker was about two hundred feet below him and to his left. They were drifting down into a wheat field just outside the village. He hoped there was a doctor who could take care of Eric. He had already resigned himself to being a prisoner for the rest of the war, but still hoped they would find someone from the resistance, even though he knew that was a long shot.

Svensen watched as Blocker hit the ground and crumpled up like a bag of meal. The air was still and his chute fell over him like a shroud; a bad omen. Just before he hit the ground, out of the corner of his eye, Svensen saw a group of villagers approaching from the far end of the field.

The villagers had distracted him and he twisted his left knee badly when he landed. Wincing in pain, he unbuckled his chute and hobbled over to where Blocker lay motionless. His friend moaned softly when he rolled him over, which meant he was still alive, but the bleeding had started again.

He had taken the plane's first aid kit with him when he jumped and he took out a morphine stick and quickly jammed it into Eric's leg, then grabbed the remaining bandages and began to rewrap the shrapnel wounds where the blood was seeping out of the old dressings. He heard a commotion behind him and turned and saw the villagers coming up over the small rise. They were almost to him.

There were twelve to fifteen of them, mostly old men with a few young boys and several women trailing behind them. They looked angry and were moving toward him with strong, purposeful strides, wielding clubs, shovels, and pitchforks. Were those weapons meant for him or were they meant to protect him from the Germans? Before he bailed out he didn't have time to get an accurate check of their position so he didn't know if he had landed in Germany or France.

When he was a kid he had seen the movie Frankenstein, starring Boris Karloff and it had scared the beejeebers out of him. Now this whole thing reminded him of the scene in the movie when the villagers stormed Dr. Frankenstein's castle. As he stood to face them, he wondered if these villagers would see him as a liberator, an invader… or as a monster? He looked down at his bleeding friend; surely they wouldn't harm an injured man, would they? He thought about drawing his pistol, but decided against it; he wasn't a monster.

The mob stopped a few feet in front of him and stared at him in silence. He could see a mixture of fear, anger and pity in their eyes. Their eyes darted back and forth between him and Blocker. The bombardier moaned softly and one of the women started to go to him but was held back by the forceful arm of the man who seemed to be in charge.

He was in his late sixties, short and stocky with a barrel chest and without an ounce of fat on him. His hair hadn't thinned with age, but it was turning white in a marked contrast to his weather-worn leathery skin. He may be older than he was, but by the fire in the villager's eyes, he knew that he would not want to fight this man.

"Am-er-i-cans," Svensen said, pointing to himself and to Eric lying on the ground. "He's hurt. He needs a doctor." Blocker moaned again and the woman moved toward him but the man stopped her again.

"He's hurt!" Svensen shouted. "Do you have a doctor here?"

No one moved, they just stood and stared. Svensen shook his head and swore under his breath as he turned to kneel down beside his friend. As he turned, he caught a flash of movement out of the corner of his eye and looked up just in time to see a club come swinging.

He didn't even have time to raise his arm when he felt a searing pain at the base of his skull. Instantly his vision blurred and everything turned red as he collapsed to the ground. He struggled to get up, but his arms and legs were numb and refused to move.

The numbness was shooting through his body and he was beginning to feel dizzy, lightheaded and nauseous all at the same time. So this is what it feels like to die, he thought. Svensen collapsed to the ground beside his friend and caught a glimpse of Eric lying next to him. The last thought he had as the numbness swept over his body and the red turned to blackness was at least he would die with his buddy.

CHAPTER FIVE

Captain Mike Perry watched as the *Red Light Lady* went into a fatal spin. He'd seen so many planes go down that way before but never thought the day would come when he would be watching his own plane plummet to the earth. With agonizing slowness, the great plane spun around and around and around for its final landing. The smoke from the engines twisted in a spiral that curled like a ribbon on a Christmas present. It was a sickening sight to watch, but he couldn't tear his eyes away.

He saw her hit the ground in slow motion. The right wing hit the ground first and crumpled into nothingness. The nose of the *Lady* was driven straight into the ground by the force of the impact and it flipped over on its back, then exploded as 600 gallons of aviation fuel ignited.

Mercifully it was over. Over for him, for the *Lady* herself, and for Tasker. Tasker had saved their lives at the cost of his own, but he knew he wasn't looking for life, but redemption.

Perry turned his attention away from the dead and toward the living. Though the six of them had jumped only seconds apart, they were now scattered over nearly a mile of sky. Thomas was almost down, landing in an open field with Ramos and Idleman not far behind.

He, Gibbler and Mitchell were evenly spaced and would land in an adjacent field about a half mile away that was separated by a small patch of forest.

As he floated down, all he could think about was his wife and what she would go through. He could just picture her sitting at home teaching their daughter to read. Alyssa was only five but she already knew all her ABCs and could even count to a hundred. They would be cuddled up together on the couch when they would hear a quiet rap on the door. Puzzled, she would get up and tell Alyssa to stay put but his curious little one would tag along and hide behind her mother's skirt when she opened the door.

Cheryl would immediately know something was wrong when she would open the door and find two men in uniform standing in front of her. The men would speak quietly and hand her the telegram that said her husband was a prisoner of war. She would start to cry and Alyssa would peek from behind her skirt and look up at her and ask what was wrong, and she would cry even harder because she couldn't tell her that something had happened to her daddy.

Perry suddenly stopped himself. At least he hoped it would say he was a POW and not killed in action; that thought had never crossed his mind until that moment. His heart ached; he hated to be the cause of so much pain to his wife and daughter.

Perry watched as Mitchell disappeared just inside the tree line and his copilot landed about 50 yards in front of him in the open field. Perry realized the he was coming down fast and tried to remember what they had taught them in flight training about bailing out and how to land. The last thing he needed now was a sprained or broken ankle.

He landed hard on his feet, throwing up a big puff of dust, and rolled once. A gust of wind caught his chute and popped him back up then dropped him again as it suddenly slackened. The momentum carried him forward and he flipped once then hit the ground landing face first, spread eagled. He lay there for a moment catching his breath, then rolled over and started gathering in his chute. By the time he had it wrapped up in his arms, Gibbler had come up.

"Nice landing, skipper," Gibbler snickered. "I'm glad you land an airplane better than you land yourself."

"Very funny." He twisted up the remaining shroud lines then started running toward the trees. "Did you see Mitchell?"

"He was right in front of me. I lost him when he went into the trees, but I think he's straight ahead, by that tall one over there," Gibbler said, pointing.

"Come on," Perry said as they headed toward the trees. The trees were sparse so it wasn't hard to find a 28 foot diameter piece of cloth tangled in their branches. Mitchell was hanging motionless about six feet above the ground like a giant Christmas ornament. Perry and Gibbler looked at each other. They both thought he was dead, but neither one wanted to say it. Just then they heard him groan.

Gibbler smiled. "Bet ya five bucks he fainted."

"No bet," Perry said as he walked over and grabbed Mitchell's foot and shook it hard. "Mitchell, wake up, wake up!" The ball turret gunner slowly came to and panicked when he opened his eyes and saw he was stuck in a tree. He began kicking his legs and kicked his captain in the jaw. Perry reeled back from the blow, but remained on his feet. Mitchell froze in terror, realizing he had just kicked his commanding officer.

"Sir, I'm so sorry, I didn't mean to kick you."

Perry rubbed his jaw while Gibbler stood by and tried not to laugh. Perry shot his copilot a dirty look. "It's okay," he said to Mitchell, "just release your harness and you'll drop down." Mitchell nodded, then released the harness and fell to the ground and amazingly stayed on his feet.

"He landed better than you did, skipper."

"Just because we're deep behind enemy lines doesn't mean I still can't have you court martialed for insubordination."

"Are we going to try and find the rest of the fellas?" Mitchell asked.

Perry shook his head. "Negative. We all stand a better chance of evading capture if we stay split up."

"I think, and hope, we're in France," Gibbler said, "but I'm not positive. Tommy wasn't exactly sure where we were when he jumped. I saw several small villages to the north and a larger town to the west. I say we head toward the villages."

"I agree," Perry said. "Less people, less reason for the Germans to have a garrison there. Besides, country folk tend to be more independent than city dwellers and are less likely to support the Germans. I think we have a better chance of finding the resistance or, at the very least, a handout on our way through. We'll stay in the forest and put as much distance between us and the crash site, then hide ourselves for the night. I think it would be too dangerous to try and move through the forest at night." They all nodded in agreement. "Good. Then let's go!"

CHAPTER SIX

Radioman Staff Sergeant Joe Thomas came down in the grassy field and quickly gathered up his chute. He couldn't think of a better or worse place to land. It was in the middle of an open field so there were no trees to worry about getting tangled up in; but being so open it offered no place to hide. For all he knew, some Kraut could have his head in the middle of his crosshairs right now. Putting that thought aside, he looked up and saw Ramos and Idleman floating down and started running toward them.

Thomas watched as the tough kid from California landed. He hit the ground, did a roll then popped back up to his feet just like he knew what he was doing. Ramos had his harness off and his chute gathered by the time Thomas got there. Idleman had landed much closer to the trees and was already in the woods waving for his friends to join him.

They jumped over the fallen log that Idleman was behind and stared at the field, catching their breath and looking for any sign that the Germans had spotted them.

"I saw a couple of hick villages a couple of miles to the north of us and what looked like a pretty good size town to the west. I say we head to the town," Ramos said.

"What do you think, Joe?" Idleman asked.

"Why do you want to head to the city, Tony?" Thomas asked.

"Any organized resistance is going to be in the city where the information flows, not in the sleepy country where the most exciting thing to happen is the neighbor's cat coughing up a fur ball. I'm a city boy, I'm from L.A. and I'm in my element in the city. I can find the people we need to contact, and besides, it'll be easier to hide in a town with ten thousand people in it than a village with only a couple of hundred. There are only so many barns and haystacks you can hide in."

Thomas thought about it for a moment. "Okay by me. The city it is then. We'll put a couple of miles between us and here, then sit tight until it's dark and travel the rest of the way at night."

CHAPTER SEVEN

After about half an hour of waiting and watching, Billy Jacobs began to move in a southwesterly direction, away from the village he'd seen. He knew he might find someone from the resistance there, but he also might find a German sympathizer and he didn't want to take that chance. At this point, he chose to rely on himself and not others.

He walked for several hours, pausing often to wait and listen, seeing if he was being tracked. As he walked, he marveled at how similar the German woods were to his forest back home. This forest was a little dryer and had less undergrowth, but all in all, he felt at home. He came across a small stream and stepped into it off some stones so as not to leave any sign. He then walked several hundred yards upstream and crawled out on a fallen log, again to throw off the scent of any dogs they might be using to track him.

Carefully, he walked along the creek bank and found the perfect campsite for his first night on the run. It was a hollowed out tree stump that was large enough for him to build a small fire inside yet not be seen and the branches of the nearby trees were close enough to disperse the smoke as it rose.

He had his knife with him and it didn't take long for him to make a couple of small spears. He found a good spot by the creek and waited patiently for a squirrel, or a wild pig if he were lucky, to come by and bang! He'd have dinner.

Looking around, he saw several fallen logs next to the stump. He could see that there was just enough room for him to crawl underneath them and cover himself with leaves. He nodded in approval; all in all, it would be like taking a camping trip back home, he told himself. He sighed; if only he could believe that.

The next morning he awoke about an hour after sunrise. The morning was a dull gray, a low lying fog covering parts of the forest. His stomach began growling, not satisfied with the one small squirrel he had managed to kill and cook last night. He told himself he would have plenty of time to hunt today and not to worry. He was just about to get up and search for breakfast when he heard a loud snap. Instantly he froze, held his breath; waiting, listening.

With sheer terror, he realized that someone was actually walking on the logs he was lying under! He could feel the logs bow from the weight of the person above him. Step by step, he followed their footsteps as they moved from his feet toward his head. Suddenly, his stomach announced it longed for more food with a long and loud gurgle that he just knew the German would hear.

The footsteps stopped. It felt like there were two people and they were perched directly above him. A thousand thoughts began rushing through his head. Did they know he was there? Should he try to reach his pistol? Would they even try to capture him or just shoot him and leave him buried there?

If his stomach didn't give him away, he knew the sound of his pounding heart would. His unseen captors stood motionless above him, then after what seemed like an eternity, he felt relief as they walked off the logs and moved away into the woods. He remained frozen, allowing them time to leave the area and time for his racing heart to slow to normal before he got up.

Cautiously he crawled out from under the logs and crouched low, surveying the area. His eyes darted about the forest, searching for any telltale sign that the Germans were still in the area. Suddenly his eyes flew open wide as he focused on a set of footprints that were next to the logs; it hadn't been a squad of German soldiers that had been standing on the logs. It was a bear.

He had thought about being captured in the woods, but not eaten. It had never occurred to him that there could be danger in the woods other than the Germans. He wondered if German bears hated Americans too.

Fortunately, the bear was not heading in the same direction he was. The sun had now broken though the morning cloud cover and its warmth felt good on his face, but he knew the good weather wouldn't last. Off to the east, he could see rain clouds marching across the sky. He figured that by late afternoon, early evening, he would have rain to contend with.

Slowly and carefully he started walking through the forest again. This time, he kept his eyes open, not only for Germans but also for any sign of wild animals. The walk in the woods was pleasant and he actually enjoyed it. He preferred nature and living in the country to life in the city, but for the past couple of years he hadn't had much of a choice. What with boot camp, training, being shipped over to England and all the missions they'd flown, he'd barely had time to check out the woods just outside of base.

Whenever they'd gotten any leave, the other guys always wanted to go into town and meet girls. Now he certainly didn't have anything against meeting a nice girl, but sometimes he could swear that that was the only thing on their minds; all except the captain of course, because he already had a family. No, he was as red blooded as the next guy, but there was just something special about being in the middle of the forest all by yourself. But unfortunately there wasn't too much open ground around base. Too many people for too many centuries had left too little "real" forestlands.

But Europe was different because it was so much bigger. He'd looked down from his tail gun position on many missions and admired the many miles of untouched forests and watched the winding threads of rivers as they cut through the wilderness. When he was up there, he wished he were walking through the trees. Now that he was here, he wished he were back up in the skies.

He was walking through a small gorge, when he heard a faint, low rumble. At first he thought it was thunder but the sound was steady and seemed to be growing louder. It was bouncing off the canyon walls and growing in intensity, flooding the valley with a rising tide of sound. The roar was deep and he could it feel it rumbling down in the pit of his stomach, and yet there seemed to be a faint, high pitched whine that his ears barely caught but couldn't identify. The noise reached a sudden crescendo as an aircraft burst into sight over the low ridge, streaking across the sky no more than 100 feet above the ground.

Its angular fuselage gave it a menacing, confident look as it raced by; looking like it owned the sky. It was a dark, matte gray that seemed to absorb the light.

Then, just as quickly as the tide had risen, the rumble drained away as the plane vanished over the next ridge.

Suddenly Jacobs realized that he had been standing in the middle of the small clearing and that the pilot easily could have seen him. He had been gawking at the plane instead of hiding as he should have. He mentally kicked himself for being so careless. He had been too caught up with his little stroll through the countryside to paying attention to what was going on. He had to remember that he was still fighting a war, and even if he enjoyed being in the woods, they were still German woods.

Jacobs continued north, weaving his way in and out of the trees. He had seen several footprints, all at least a week old. The tracks appeared to belong to just one person and not a squad of soldiers, which made him feel a little better. But it also meant that it was probably a hunter out looking for game and that also meant he would be carrying a gun, so he would still have to be very careful.

Off in the distance he saw a faint wisp of smoke. His growling stomach told him to take the chance and head for it. He was hoping it was a farmhouse where he might be able to steal some food. The small squirrel that he ate last night just wasn't cutting it. Even though he was starving, he still took his time, being very diligent about watching for any sign that someone might be watching him.

To his delight, he found a small farmhouse sitting in a clearing. The front of the house faced two open fields that were ready for plowing and a stand of timber surrounded the back. From his hiding position in the trees, Jacobs could also see a small barnyard with a few chickens running around, three pigs in a pen, two cows and an old plow horse. Fortunately he didn't see any dogs. Later that night he would have to sneak into the coop and relieve the chickens of a few of their eggs.

He crouched behind a tree and continued to watch the house. A woman in her early forties emerged from the house and hung clothes on a line to dry. She was humming as she worked and Jacobs thought the tune sounded familiar. It took him a moment but he finally recognized it as a song he'd heard on the German propaganda radio show *Lord Haw Haw*.

Since she knew the song too, did that mean she was a German or a German sympathizer or that she had just listened to the radio like he had? In either case, he knew he would have to be careful. She continued working for a few more minutes then disappeared into the house.

Moments later she appeared at the window and she set a freshly baked loaf of bread on the sill to cool. It was pure torture for him to smell the bread and he could even see the steam rising from it. There was nothing the Germans could do to him right now that would be worse than seeing and smelling the bread and not being able to eat it. His stomach was shouting at him to sneak up and take it, but his brain knew better. Right now though, his stomach was beginning to win the fight.

His attention was diverted to a man who came walking down the side of the field closest to the house. He was carrying a shotgun in one hand and two wild turkeys in the other. He looked to be in his late forties, wearing overalls and a narrow brimmed hat.

Looking north, Jacobs could see more scattered threads of smoke curling upward, dotting the countryside. To the west he saw several large columns of heavy smoke rising from industrial areas. He could see that he wouldn't be able to totally avoid people any longer, which meant that just as in the forest, he would have to blend in with his environment to survive; he would have to find some civilian clothes.

He didn't want to stay in any one place for too long, but he felt like he should stay here because it was his perfect opportunity to get both a set of new clothes and something to eat. The man looked to be about his size and the woman had just hung several sets of shirts and pants out on the clothesline.

Reluctantly, he abandoned the idea of stealing the bread and crawled in between several large boulders, then piled some dead branches over himself to help him hide, and settled down to wait until nightfall.

It was just after dusk when Jacobs decided to make his move. His plan was to crawl out, grab the clothes, raid the chicken coop, then get back into the woods and run. He was going to grab a shirt and a pair of pants and he also was going to grab some of the women's clothes. He figured that if he took her stuff too, it would divert suspicion by making it look more like it was taken by a local or a passing gypsy than by a downed American airman.

The night was still and he could swear he sounded like a Sherman tank crawling along the ground. He crawled on his belly to the side of the house, then snaked his way to the corner. He pressed against the house, sweating and listening to learn if he had been discovered. There was no movement from inside so he got up his courage to crawl across the dirt and grab the clothes.

Without warning, the back door suddenly opened and a path of light spilled out of the house and flooded into the backyard. The woman came out of the house with her laundry basket tucked up underneath her arm and she nearly stepped on him as she walked by. Her eyes, still accustomed to the light, didn't see a man lying in her yard, just a dark patch on the ground.

What should I do? Jacobs thought. Should I run and take my chances or just lie still and hope she won't see me? Back home hunting, the game that got spooked and was flushed out was usually the one that got shot. He decided to stay where he was and hope that the luck that had been with him so far would hold out just a little bit longer.

The woman hummed quietly to herself as she took down the clothes, then folded and placed them in the basket. There was something about the tune that seemed familiar to him, but perhaps he was just homesick. It was chilly out and she started to hurry, taking them down and putting them in the basket without folding them. Just a few more moments and it will all be over, Jacobs told himself.

Finally she had the last shirt in her hand, hastily threw it in her basket and started walking back to the house. Jacobs began to panic when he realized that she was walking straight towards him. Four more steps and she would be on him. Three steps, two, and at the last second Jacobs rolled on his side as her foot came down where the middle of his back had been.

The woman must have seen him move because she suddenly screamed. To make matters worse, she was so startled that she lost her balance and fell on top of him, covering him in a shower of clothes, flailing arms and legs. He tried to calm her down and get her to stop screaming but she was too scared to listen. He tried to cover her mouth but that only made it worse and he let out his own scream as she nearly bit his little finger in two.

Jacobs had just managed to roll the frightened woman off him when he heard the most unmistakable sound in the world; the ratcheting shuck of a shotgun shell being loaded into the chamber. In a split second, he had to make a decision — stay or run? It was dark and the scene chaotic with the poor woman screaming. Perhaps the farmer would hold his fire because his wife was so close, allowing him to slip into the darkness. But then again, the farmer was very close and the image of him carrying the two dead turkeys filled his mind.

He rolled over on the ground and placed his hands over his head and shouted over and over again, "I'm an American, don't shoot!" The woman scampered away and retreated behind the safety of her husband. Slowly, with the gun raised, the farmer stepped out of the back door and approached the stranger who had attacked his wife.

Cautiously, the farmer moved forward then stopped. "American?" he said in very broken English.

"Yes, yes!" Jacobs replied, relief pouring through his words. "ME A-MER-I-CA-N." He slowly got to his knees and then reached inside his shirt and pulled out his dog tags. "See, American."

The farmer looked skeptical, but motioned with his gun for Jacobs to go into the house. Jacobs obliged, walked slowly with hands raised high through the back door then sat down at the table. "That bread sure smelled mighty good this afternoon, ma'am. Might I trouble you for just a small piece of it? I haven't had anything to eat for nearly two days, except for a little squirrel I killed. I'd sure be awful obliged to you."

The man and the woman just looked at each other. It was clear that they didn't understand a word that their surprise guest had said. They replied, spewing out words faster than a submachine gun. Jacobs' eyes were filled with the same puzzled look as his hosts'.

Jacobs took his hands and pretended to be eating out of a bowl to get his point across that he was hungry. He even pointed to the bread that was sitting on the counter.

The woman smiled, and got a plate and gave her hungry visitor a large slice. "Thank you, ma'am," Jacobs said with a smile that matched the size of the slice of bread. The famished American tried not to be rude and show bad manners by devouring his food too fast, but he just couldn't help it, the entire slice disappeared in four huge bites. The woman smiled, but the farmer still had a poker face.

The man grunted, then waved his gun, motioning for Jacobs to go back outside. He hesitated just outside the door but was spurred on by the barrel of the shotgun shoved between his shoulder blades. They marched silently into the darkness and away from the comfort and warmth of the farmhouse. Where was the farmer taking him? Was he the condemned man who had just had his last meal and was now being taken to be turned over to the Gestapo or worse?

He thought about making a break for it, but he had seen the look in the farmer's eyes; the man may be older, but he was a hunter and Jacobs knew he wouldn't miss, even in the dark. They walked in silence for what seemed like miles when they came to another farmhouse. The lights were out, but that didn't stop the old man from walking up and pounding on the door.

The man who opened the door was younger than the farmer and just stared at him and at Jacobs. Soon, the two men were engaged in a heated conversation that bordered on anger as both men gestured wildly with their hands, pointing at Jacobs. After a few minutes, the older man just turned and walked away, leaving Jacobs standing there alone with the other. He didn't know if that was a good or bad thing.

"What is your name?" the man finally asked in fairly good English.

"Staff Sergeant Billy, I mean Jacobs, William H., serial number 6335148."

"And where did you come from?"

"I was shot down yesterday."

"Your target and bomber group you are with?

"I'm afraid I can't tell you that," Jacobs hesitated. "All I'm supposed to give is my name, rank and serial number."

"You might be a Nazi spy, sent to infiltrate the resistance and turn us all into the Gestapo. If you can prove who you are and that you're not a spy, then maybe I could help you."

Jacobs stood silent, weighing his options. "I'm sorry, sir," he finally said, shaking his head. "I ain't no Nazi spy but I ain't gonna tell you anything other than my name, rank and serial number. If you think me a spy, then so be it. But I ain't telling you nothing."

The man paused and looked at Jacobs for a moment. "Tell, do you know the words to your national anthem?"

"The Star Spangled Banner? Yeah, sure."

"Can you sing all three verses and prove to me that you are an American?"

Jacobs paused, a look of embarrassment covering his face. "I didn't know there were three verses to it."

The Frenchman smiled. "There aren't three verses, there are four. If you were a spy, the Germans in their usual efficient manner, would have taught you all four verses and you would have proudly sung them to me to prove you were a good American, and then I would have had to kill you as a spy. You see, most of you Americans only know the one verse."

The man stepped aside and opened the door and motioned to Jacobs. "Come inside, William, we have much to talk about."

CHAPTER EIGHT

Tommy Svensen was sure he was dead and that he must be in Hell by the way his head hurt. Slowly he opened his eyes and found that he was neither in Heaven or Hell. It was dark and he was leaning against a building facing the town square. He tried to move his arms and legs but they refused to cooperate.

When he had first bailed out, he didn't know if he had landed in France or Germany, but looking down at the ropes that tightly held his hands and legs in check, it looked like Germany. He struggled briefly, but every time he moved, the pounding in his head doubled.

There was a small fire in the middle of the square and it was surrounded by a large crowd, and they didn't look too friendly. The old man who had hit him earlier was walking around the fire, waving his hands in the air, as if to give special meaning to each word he said. Occasionally, another villager would speak, but then the old man would cut him down with his reply. Svensen couldn't hear clearly what they were saying; only bits and pieces, but it didn't matter anyway since he didn't understand German. He couldn't hear their words, but he was sure that he was the main topic of discussion.

Suddenly he noticed a shadowy figure lurking off to the side. It stood there for a moment then slowly moved forward. The figure emerged into the light, revealing a little girl. She must have been about eight or nine, he guessed, and he noticed that she was staring at him with a great deal of curiosity. She stood there for the longest time, just staring and examining him. Finally she broke her silence.

"Did you kill my father?" she asked in perfect English.

Svensen just sat there in shock. Shocked at the question itself and shocked that she asked it in English. After a moment, he replied, "Why would you think that I killed your father?"

"My father didn't come home two nights ago. Two men who wore uniforms just like his came to our village and told us that he wouldn't be coming home ever again. Mother has been crying ever since. They said he died a glorious death defending the Fatherland from an American bomber attack."

Svensen studied the little girl for a moment. She seemed very grown up for her age and she asked the question not out of hate, seeking revenge on her father's killer, but with a genuine interest in the answer and knowing the truth.

"What's your name?" he asked.

"Greta."

"Hi, Greta. My name is Tommy," Svensen replied, trying to put on the biggest smile he could muster under the circumstances. "Was your father a fighter pilot?"

"Yes, he flew the Messerschmitt 109. He said he flew in the Folk Wulf 190 but said it was a big ugly beast that flew like a brute. Even though the 190 was faster, he says he preferred the style and grace of the 109. On Sundays, even though he wasn't supposed to, he would sneak me onto the airfield and take me up for rides. It was so pretty way up there. We would fly over our village and I would look down and wave at my mother. She looked like a little bug from way up there, but that was a long time ago. When I grow up I want to be a pilot and fly airplanes just like my father."

Svensen's smile faded with the girl's story. He was used to seeing the war from 20,000 feet—not up close and not like this. "War is very confusing," Svensen started out slowly. "Things happen very fast. We shoot at them and they shoot at us. It's hard to know exactly who hit who. So, to answer your question, I can't really say if it was our plane or another who shot your father down."

Greta stood there and seemed to accept the answer. Just then he heard loud shouts coming from the meeting. "What are they talking about?" Svensen asked.

"You," she said very matter-of-factly.

"What are they saying?"

"They are trying to decide what to do with you." By now she had come closer and was standing right in front of him, about five feet away, looking at him like he was a display piece in a museum. "Some of the people want to turn you over to the soldiers while others simply want to kill you."

Svensen was taken aback by her matter-of-fact answer and that death was something she was so used to at her age. "The old man, he seems to be the leader here, what does he want to do?"

"That's Grandpapa; he wants to kill you and be done with it. He says it will be easier than waiting for the soldiers to come. Grandpapa hates the British and Americans and blames them for starting the war."

"But we didn't start the war, your Hitler did."

Greta just shrugged her shoulders

"What about my friend? Is he all right?"

"No, I think I heard them say he died, something about him losing too much blood. They're even arguing about that too. Some want to bury him in the village cemetery since he died here, while others just want to burn the body outside of the village."

"What do you think they should do with me?" Svensen asked. But before she could answer, the girl's mother saw her talking to the captive American and came running over.

"Greta! Get away from him!" she shouted. She ran over and grabbed the child in her arms like she was snatching her from the jaws of death.

"We were just talking, ma'am. You have a very bright and lovely daughter." He paused for a moment then continued. "And I'm sorry to hear about your husband."

She smiled weakly, trying to keep wounds closed that were still too fresh and too deep. A simple "Thank you" was all she could manage. She clutched the child even tighter now, more for support than to protect. After a moment, she spoke again. "And I am sorry about your friend, he died late this afternoon. We did try to help him, but he had lost too much blood."

"Thank you, I appreciate your efforts."

In the far distance, the sound of gunfire could be heard. The thunderclaps of heavy artillery rolled across the night sky followed by the faint echo of machine gun fire. By the sounds of it, the gathering storm was getting closer. For a moment, they both stopped to watch the distant flashes of the exploding shells.

"They are not far off," the woman said, her voice suddenly heavy. "They should be here by noon tomorrow at the latest."

"And what of me?"

"There is a small garrison a few kilometers from here. We will turn you over to them in the morning."

"I see," Svensen said, relieved that they were going to turn him in rather than kill him. Suddenly his stomach began rumbling like the distant artillery. "Would it be possible to get something to eat? I haven't eaten anything since early this morning."

"Yes, just a moment." She walked back over to where they had had the meeting. Most of the villagers had left by now with just a few still lingering around the fire. Some were poking and prodding at it while others talked quietly, glancing every so often at the bound American flyer. The woman picked up a small basket and returned.

She approached the airman cautiously and opened the basket and knelt down beside him. She took out a small, half loaf of bread and started to tear off a piece to give to him when suddenly there was a shout. She stood up quickly and spun around. The old man, Grandpapa, came running over. He slapped the bread out of her hand and began scolding her.

"Helga, how can you even think of giving this man anything to eat when half the village is starving!" he shouted in German. "We barely have enough for ourselves and you want to waste it on the enemy? What kind of example is this to show your daughter, especially after your husband was killed by the likes of him? You will leave him now. We will take him to the garrison in the morning and let them feed him. "

"Yes, Papa," she said, glaring back at him. "And what kind of an example are we setting for Greta? He is a person, not an animal to be tied up and left behind the barn. We should set an example of compassion by allowing him the simplest of human dignity by permitting him to eat and at least have a blanket."

"No, I absolutely forbid it!"

The two locked stares for a moment and then the woman finally relented and started to walk away, but before she did, she turned and looked at the American and softly said, "I'm sorry." She reached out and took Greta's hand and began walking toward the end of the village. The little girl turned and looked at the man tied up against the wall until they disappeared into the night.

As soon as the two had vanished into the night, the old man turned and kicked Svensen in the legs. Svensen looked up and saw two eyes full of hatred staring down at him. Svensen wanted to hate this man but all he could feel was pity. The German must have sensed that and kicked him again. Svensen cringed in pain and tried to curl up in a ball to protect himself. More kicks came; they were strong, but not accurate.

"Swine," he said in broken English. "If I had my way, you would be dead by now."

"Why do you hate me so much? What have I ever done to you?"

"Why? Because you are the enemy. You come over here and bomb our towns and villages, kill our sons and you ask me why I hate you?"

"But what have I done to you?"

The old man didn't like the question so he kicked him two more times and stormed off into the night.

"Keep your mouth shut next time," Svensen told himself. A gentle breeze came up and wound its way through the streets of the village. Chilled by the night air, Svensen brought his knees up to his chest for warmth and with the echoing of gunfire ringing in the distance, he drifted off into a restless, fitful sleep.

The morning light didn't bring Lt. Svensen's liberation, only numbness and pain in his arms and legs from the ropes. He desperately wanted to stretch, to shake the weariness from his body and give his muscles a chance to move, but the ropes were still tight. He raised his head to look around and thought what a strange prison he was in.

A rooster perched on a fence post on the edge of the village crowed as the first rays of light poked up over the horizon. Soon people began to trickle out from their homes. He heard the cackle of hens when an old woman emerged from a chicken pen after gathering their eggs for breakfast.

He watched as a little boy of no more than five stumbled out of a doorway with a metal bucket in hand, wiping the sleep from his eyes. He walked over to the family cow, set the bucket down, yawed and stretched, then crawled under the cow and began milking it. He was soon joined by two puppies that came tumbling out of the barn. The boy took careful aim and he took turns trying to shoot milk into their mouths. This lasted until a sharp rebuke from his mother sent the puppies scurrying for cover and the boy sat up and began aiming the milk into the bucket.

He looked over to his right and saw a tiny head peering around the corner. She ducked back behind the corner then came running out. Running all the way, she dropped to her knees in front of the tied up American. "I wanted to get here before Grandpapa woke up," she said, panting and trying to catch her breath. "Here." She took out a piece of bread from under her coat.

It was just a piece of bread, but to him it looked like a banquet. She held it up and he took a big bite. It was fresh and still warm from the oven; it was the best bread he had ever tasted in his life. She had torn off another piece and was about to give it to him when she was stopped by a loud voice that echoed through the small square.

"Greta! Stop that right now!" the old man shouted and came running toward them. Sensing his breakfast was over he leaned forward and snapped at the bread like a coiled snake. He grabbed the bread in his mouth and started chewing as fast as he could. The little girl squealed in surprise and fell backwards.

"Swine!" he shouted. "You hurt her!" But before Greta could say anything, the old man brought his right fist down hard on the American, sending him sprawling as much as the ropes would allow. Last night, Svensen didn't hate the old man, but that was quickly changing.

"I didn't hurt her!" he shouted back.

"Yes, you did!" he shouted back and then kicked him in the legs.

"Grandpapa, stop! Please stop! He didn't hurt me; he just scared me, that's all." She wrapped herself around her grandfather's legs and held onto them to keep him from kicking, but the old man was so full of rage, he reached down and pried her fingers away then threw her on the ground and started kicking the prisoner again. Years of frustration, hurt, and anger all boiled to the surface and the old man was taking the entire war out on the only enemy he could find.

Suddenly the air was split with the sound of rifle fire that was close, just on the other side of the river. Everyone and everything in the village stopped, including the beating, as they listened. Machine gun fire now peppered the air, punctuated by the sound of mortar rounds exploding. Drifting between the gunfire and explosions could be heard the faint, yet unmistakable sound of clanging metal. Tanks were coming.

Everyone stood mesmerized by the sound of the approaching battle. They'd all heard the rumblings of battle before, but it had always been far away and over the horizon. But now, instead of being over the horizon, it was just over the hill.

Looking north toward the sounds, they saw a trail of dust rapidly drawing near. Soon they heard the sounds of truck engines and then shouts. To the villagers' relief, the soldiers were speaking German, but the relief soon turned to panic.

Dozens of German soldiers came running through the village now. There was no rank, no order or formation; they were in a panicked, headlong retreat, running as fast as they could. All the villagers just stood in stunned disbelief as they watched their mighty army pass by them in a running parade.

The old man grabbed a young lieutenant by the arm as he ran by.

"What is going on? Why are you running?"

"The Russians are just over the ridge and we can't stop them. Run for your lives!"

"But we have an American prisoner here. We wish to turn him over to you."

"Didn't you hear me?" the lieutenant shouted as he turned to face the villagers. "The Russian army is less than a kilometer from here and they have destroyed everything and everyone in their path. They have a bloodlust for revenge. Run and run now!" He shook his arm free from the old man's grip then took off running again.

"What's wrong?" Svensen asked as Greta and her mother both ran over and started untying his ropes.

"Those are Russian guns coming over the hill and the lieutenant says they are taking no prisoners. The Russians hate us and will not think twice about killing everyone in the village. We've got to try to escape."

Just then a tank shell exploded on the far end of the village causing everyone to bury their heads. When they looked up, they were all covered in dust and dirt. "Come on, everyone!" Helga shouted. "We've got to hurry!"

The old man picked up a rifle that one of the soldiers had dropped and walked over to the American.

"Move, Helga," he ordered as he brought back the bolt on the rifle and put a cartridge in the chamber and pointed the rifle at the young flyer.

"No!" she shouted with such force that it surprised the old man. "I know he was your son, but he was my husband too and I will miss him for the rest of my life. But killing this American will not bring Ernst back. There has been enough killing."

Svensen stood to his feet and rubbed his wrists where the ropes had been. His legs were wobbly but he stood as firm as he could.

Just then several more tank rounds fell behind the village, cutting off their retreat.

"We're trapped," Helga said, fear clearly showing in her eyes. Fear not so much for herself, but for her daughter. "There is no way out and no place to hide."

With a look of the utmost sadness, the old man pulled an old rusty revolver out of his coat pocket and handed it to Helga. "You know what to do with this," he said in a low and quiet voice. Then with a tone of new, redirected anger he said, "I will take as many of those Cossacks with me as possible."

"No," Svensen said, "I have an idea. It's a long shot but it's the only one we've got." He walked over and took the revolver from Helga then grabbed for the old man's rifle, but he refused to give it up.

"Let him have it," Helga said sternly. Seeing the determination in his daughter's eyes, he reluctantly gave it to the American. Svensen tucked the revolver in his waistband then grabbed the rifle. He turned to Helga.

"Okay, tell everyone in the village to get into a group and get behind me. Make sure that they don't have weapons of any kind."

Helga turned and relayed Svensen's instructions to the frightened villagers. They were bewildered and didn't understand, but followed his orders anyway. By now the shooting had stopped, but they could hear the clanking of the advancing tank.

Finally they saw it. A Russian T-34 tank, flanked on either side by a dozen soldiers, crested the top of the hill and headed straight for the village. The tank stopped thirty feet in front of the villagers, and the top hatch opened and a Russian captain appeared. There was no hiding his surprise to see a town full of Germans standing behind a single American soldier. He looked over the strange group, then smiled.

"Thank you, Lieutenant, for rounding them all up for us," the Russian said in broken English. "But we will take over from here."

"Begging the Captain's pardon, but these are my prisoners and under the jurisdiction and protection of the United States Army."

The Russian laughed. "Yes, yes, I will be sure to mention your name in my report. Now step aside."

"No, sir," Svensen replied, trying to sound more confident and in charge than he felt. "Take whatever supplies you want from the village, but the prisoners stay with me."

The captain gave him a dismissive look, then waved his hand for his troops to move in. Svensen chambered a round then fired it into the air. The Russian soldiers froze in their tracks, looking to their captain for orders. "I said these were my prisoners and under my protection!" Svensen shouted again.

The smile vanished from the captain's face and was replaced by a cold, hard stare. "We will take whatever we want, Lieutenant. Now I said step aside or you will die along with your prisoners."

"No, sir!"

"Is everything all right, Lieutenant?" came a shout from across the river. Everyone's heads snapped as they turned to see who had spoken. While they had been talking, three US Sherman tanks and a company of infantry had slipped into the burned out part of the village on the other side of the river. Svensen looked at the American tanks then back to the Russian captain and smiled. "Yes, sir, everything is just fine. The captain and I were just having a friendly little chat."

The Russian captain quickly sized up the situation. An American major was halfway out of the hatch of the lead tank while the other two tanks were buttoned up and ready for action. The soldiers were walking around casually, but were in good position to take cover and fire.

The Russian captain smiled. "Yes, I was just thanking your lieutenant here for saving me the trouble of writing up all the paperwork for the capture of this village. It is all yours, we are on our way to Berlin!" He gave the signal and all his men began moving on down the road. The tank started up and drove past Svensen and the others. As it drove by, the captain looked at Svensen. "I don't know if you are very foolish or very brave, but one thing I do know... you are very lucky."

Svensen stood on shaking legs as he watched the tank and the rest of the Russian soldiers disappeared down the road.

"We'll be across the river in a couple of hours!" the major shouted. "The Corps of Engineers is right behind us with a pontoon bridge."

"Thank you, sir," Svensen replied, then looked around; he needed to find a place to sit down before he collapsed. He walked over and sat down on the corner of the fountain in the village square. It was empty, but in relatively good shape considering the destruction that surrounded it. He took a deep breath and blew it out slowly, trying to let his nerves settle. Helga and Greta came and sat down beside him.

"Why? Why did you do that? Why did you risk your life to save ours, especially after the way we treated you?"

He hung his head down in exhaustion and drew another deep breath. "It's like you said, there's been enough killing." What he didn't tell her was that if he had been responsible for taking the life of the son in battle, the husband and father of these three people, then this was his way of making atonement by making sure his family survived.

CHAPTER NINE

The downed airmen fell exhausted just outside the small farmhouse. The sun had just settled behind the ridge and long shadows were reaching out, covering everything in sight. They watched the house from the safety of a thicket at the edge of the field and everything was quiet except for the pounding of their hearts and their gasps for breath.

The house looked like a typical farmhouse, Perry thought, much like ones he'd seen while flying over England and France, and not all that different from the ones he'd seen in Nebraska and Iowa when he was growing up. The shades were pulled down tight to keep the light from escaping but thin ribbons of light leaked from the seams, silhouetting the windows with tiny slivers of light.

The barn was unremarkable with a chicken coop on the side, a horse plow sitting beside it, and the muffled sounds of animals could be heard through the gaps in the siding.

"Sir, are we going to sleep in the barn tonight?" Mitchell asked.

Perry shook his head. "No, we need to be cautious and check things out in the morning. For all we know, there could be a squad of Germans soldiers bivouacking there." Perry could see the disappointment on his ball turret gunner's face.

"I know, it's going to get cold tonight and I'd like to sleep on a nice bed of hay myself, but we can't take the chance. We'll take three hour shifts; I'll take the first watch. Now you two go cover yourselves up with leaves and branches and be sure to sleep on your stomachs, that way you won't snore."

"Yes, sir," their weary replies came in unison as the two men slipped away into the night.

Perry sat alone in the dark. It was quiet and peaceful now; a far cry from what had happened just a few short hours ago. He wondered about Tommy and Eric and how they had made out. He was sure they had been captured and hoped Eric was still alive, but he had his doubts. And what of the others —Jacobs, Thomas, Idleman and Ramos? Had they all gotten down safely and were they still free, or had the Germans captured them?

He sat watching as the moon began to climb, peeking through the trees. A few high scattered clouds, glowing pale white from the reflected moonlight, drifted lazily drifted across the dark sky. One by one the stars were coming out, each becoming more brilliant than the one before.

How beautiful it all is, he thought. He sighed, missing his wife now more than he ever had. A thousand thoughts rushed into his head. Would he ever see her again? What if the war drew on for a couple more years? What if he couldn't get back to England and spent all that time dodging the Germans?

If he were declared dead or missing in action, would she wait for him? Would she be patient and wait and see, or would she move on and try and find a father for their daughter? He would want her to be happy but not to give him up for dead too soon. He clenched his teeth and began to feel his anger building. Just the thought of his wife with someone else made his temples throb.

Fool, he told himself. I haven't even been down a whole day and yet have my wife off and married. At least the anger was helping to keep him awake. It had been a very long day and now it was going to be a very long night.

He looked over at the farmhouse. Who was inside? he wondered. Were they in Germany or France? Even if they were in France, would they be sympathetic and help them out or would they turn them over to the Germans? Even if they were friendly, would they even be able to communicate with one another? Right now he wished he had listened to his mother when he was in high school and taken French instead of wood shop.

He shook his head again; too much thinking. Right now all he needed to worry about was staying awake and getting through the night. What he wouldn't give for a steaming cup of hot coffee right now. He learned against a tree and watched and listened.

"Skipper, wake up," Gibbler said softly as he shook his captain by the shoulder.

"Is it my turn to stand watch again already?"

"It's morning, sir, you've been asleep for over seven hours."

"Can't be," Perry protested. "I just shut my eyes." He sat up and rubbed his eyes. He looked at his watch in disbelief, hoping his copilot was wrong. Just then he caught a whiff of the most delicious aroma he had ever smelled—coffee! He could tell that it was hand ground and was as black as night. He took a deep breath, inhaling the smell as if it were a fragrant flower. And then as if it couldn't get any better, he caught the sweet smell of bacon just beginning to sizzle in the pan. He hadn't really been hungry up until now, but the smell of coffee and bacon hit him like a prizefighter's best one-two punch. His stomach growled and churned, demanding to be fed.

"That smells mighty good," Mitchell said.

"Amen to that," Gibbler agreed.

All three men were in a trance, mesmerized by the smell of the food. Suddenly a dog started barking and they were instantly brought back to reality. Was it barking at them? Just then the door to the small farmhouse opened and an old man in his early seventies wearing dirty coveralls stepped onto the porch and called the dog.

The dog came running up to his master with its tail wagging. The old man patted the dog on the head, then the animal ran back down the road, barking all the way.

"At least he's not barking at us," Gibbler said.

"Yeah, he's barking at them," Perry pointed down the road. At the far end of the dirt road, they heard a faint rumbling and followed a trail of dust as it drew closer and soon two 6x6 troop transports appeared between the trees.

"Do you think they're after us?" Mitchell said, panic clearly rising in his voice.

"I don't think so," Perry replied.

"Shouldn't we run anyway?"

Again, Perry shook his head. "If they knew where we were, they would have picked us up last night. I don't think they're kind enough to give us a good night's sleep before they take us prisoner. Let's just sit tight and watch."

The two trucks pulled up and stopped in front of the farmhouse. The driver got out of the first truck and stood and stretched. A good sign that they're not here looking for us, Perry thought. An officer got out of the passenger side and slowly walked around to the front of the vehicle. He surveyed the farm, as if sizing it up for some hidden purpose.

Eight troopers got out of each truck and began stretching and milling around the barnyard. Their uniforms were dirty and unkempt, and the soldiers all looked tired and worn, as if they had driven all night. The old man came out on the porch and his wife soon joined him.

The farmer stepped down off the porch and began talking to the officer. The conversation soon turned one-sided as the old man tried to protest but was soon silenced as two of the soldiers grabbed him. With a tilt of the officer's head, another held the farmer's wife while several more soldiers entered their house.

The downed airmen could hear crashing and banging coming from inside as the soldiers started looting the house. The old man struggled in vain against his captors while his wife stood still and wept. A few moments later the soldiers reappeared, carrying armloads of food and a few personal items that looked to be made of silver. The soldiers attacked the food, devouring it like a pack of hungry wolves. By the looks of things, some of them hadn't eaten in days.

The officer walked toward the barn, then motioned for his men to bring the farmer. A look of sheer terror raced across his wife's face. She began to struggle and scream. The soldier holding her was about to hit her but was stopped by a raised hand from the officer. Clearly disappointed, the soldier continued to hold her, but stuck a rag in her mouth. The officer frowned but did nothing as he turned and entered the barn, followed by the two guards dragging the farmer.

The woman stopped struggling and fell to her knees, sobbing gently as her eyes never strayed away from the barn door. Suddenly her sobs turned into a hysterical scream that could be heard even through the gag, as a single gunshot rang out from the barn.

The shot startled even the Americans watching safely from the woods. Perry had arrived in London after the bombings had stopped and though he had seen the effects of the war in the crumpled and twisted buildings, he had never really witnessed the brutality that it wreaked on the civilian population until now. He had thoughts of pulling out his .45 and drawing a bead on the German officer when he came out, but he knew that was pointless. Still he felt he had to do something.

The barn doors slowly opened and the officer walked out, pistol in hand. He took a cloth out of his pocket and casually, yet meticulously wiped down the gun. With a wave of his fingers he summoned two more soldiers.

Suddenly, the farmer's wife leaped to her feet and with surprising speed raced toward the barn and threw her arms around her husband who had just walked out. They stood there holding each other and crying together while the two guards carried out a pig they had just shot.

They threw the dead animal in the back of the second truck as the officer ordered all the soldiers back into the vehicles. Just before he got back in his truck, the German officer went up to the couple, snapped his heels and tilted his hat as if to say thank you, then got in and drove off.

Perry hung his head in relief, amazed at how much he had been caught up in the drama. "Well, I think this tells us we are in occupied France and not Germany. I can't see them doing that to one of their own countrymen," Perry said.

"I agree, but now what?" Gibbler said.

"We ask for help," he replied very matter-of-factly. "You two stay here though, just in case, and don't come out of hiding unless I tell you to." Perry skirted around the tree line and came out from behind the barn. He didn't want to give his friends position away if things didn't work out. The woman saw him first and grabbed her husband by the arm and spun him around. Perry walked up slowly with hands raised. "American," he said, pointing to himself. "American."

Suddenly the look of hatred and distrust was replaced by hope and joy. They ran up and embraced him. She showered him with kisses on the cheek while the farmer pumped his hand like a politician running for office. They started jumping up and down and dancing, mimicking him in saying American, American, then they also started shouting, "libéré! libéré!"

Perry couldn't figure out why they were dancing when all of a sudden it hit him; they thought he was there to liberate them. It took him a moment to get their attention.

"No, no," he said, frantically shaking his head. "No liberator, American pilot." He pointed to himself. "I was shot down, I need your help." He stuck his arms out and waved them around like he was an airplane. He felt foolish doing that, but it was the only way he could think of to get his point across. Then he pointed his fingers like guns and "shot" them. Ratatatatat. Then he put his arms out again, then "crashed."

The old coupled looked at each other, then it finally dawned on them what he was trying to say. Disappointment flooded their eyes, but there was also understanding as they began to nod their heads. Realizing that he was getting through, Perry took it one step further.

"Resistance? Maquis?" he said, with his best French accent, thinking it might help get the words across. The farmer and his wife both looked at each other with some apprehension. Perry could tell that they knew something about the resistance but weren't about to admit it, at least not yet. Finally the woman said something to him. He just smiled and shook his head, not understanding.

She smiled and held one hand like a bowl and pretended to eat out of it with the other. Perry politely shook his head. Even though his stomach was thrilled at the very thought of food, he couldn't accept it, not after what he'd just seen. He looked around, indicating to them he knew about the Germans and what they'd done, then he shook his head no again.

She waved him to come in, with a grandmotherly smile that said, 'don't argue with me young man, just come in.' He said no again, then pointed to the woods. Sheepishly, Mitchell and Gibbler stood up and gave a weak wave. The old woman's smile never faded as she waved for the others to join them. She took the young American captain's arm, gently and reassuringly patted it, then led him into the house.

CHAPTER TEN

The old farmer returned from the barn carrying four eggs that the ransacking Germans had missed. He gave them to his wife who scrambled them in what was left of the bacon grease. She opened the front of the kitchen stove and threw in a small log, then put a pot of water on the burner. The old man left the room then returned a few minutes later with a loaf of black bread. By now the water was boiling and the old woman produced a small metal can from the cupboard. The moment she opened it, Perry knew exactly what it was—coffee!

When she handed him the steaming cup, he just sat there and inhaled the aroma. For the briefest of moments there was no war, no Germans, nothing at all but the intoxicating bouquet of the coffee. He took a sip and savored it and the moment. Then she brought over the eggs, the bread, and a pitcher of fresh milk and set it on the table. Even though it had been only 24 hours since they'd eaten, it seemed like an eternity and the food set before them looked like a banquet for a king.

All manners were forgotten as they greedily attacked the food, stuffing handfuls of bread into their mouths. Perry looked up from the feeding frenzy and noticed that their hosts were not eating. Suddenly he realized that they were truly being gracious hosts and had given them their own food. He stopped shoveling the food and reached over and hit his companions on the arm. Each looked up to see what was so important that it dare interrupt their feeding.

Guilt quickly overcame the trio and they pushed away from the table. Hurt filled the old woman's eyes as her guests got up, leaving food on their plates. She tried to coax them back to the table, but this time they wouldn't budge.

Perry walked over to the woman and escorted her to the table and pulled the chair out for her to sit. At first she resisted, pretending that she wasn't hungry, but Perry refused to give in. Gibbler walked over and acted like a waiter and gestured for the farmer to sit. The couple finally sat down, touched by the show of kindness of these strangers they had met only minutes before.

After eating, the farmer tried talking to the airmen but frustration built on both sides as neither could understand what the other was saying. Finally he stood and led them outside. Once outside, he stooped down and picked up a stick and began drawing in the dirt. He drew a crude barn and pointed to it, then pointed to his barn. Then he sketched out several small houses and pointed off down the road, then drew another building with a cross on top. Perry finally understood; they were to hide in the woods while the farmer went into the nearby village and got the priest, figuring he could speak English.

Perry nodded and smiled in understanding. The three of them quickly disappeared into the woods while the farmer walked away toward the village.

The sun was at its high point when the trio spotted a horse drawn carriage coming down the road with two riders in it. The carriage came to a stop in front of the farmhouse. Driving the cart was a parish priest dressed in a traditional long frock and wearing a wide brimmed black hat. The farmer was next to him and stood on the floorboard, scanning the forest for his newfound friends. A large smile filled his face as he saw the three emerge from the woods. Moments later they were once again seated around the farmer's table.

"I'm Father Henri Leclerc," the priest said with a genuine smile and only a slight accent.

Perry shook his hand and introduced himself and the rest of his crew.

"Where did you learn to speak such good English, Father?" Perry asked.

"My family's ancestry is originally from this area but I grew up in Chicago. When I heard the Church was doing restoration work here, I jumped at the chance. That was ten years ago and I've been here ever since. The only thing I really miss is baseball. Do you think the Cardinals can win it all again this year?"

"I don't know, Father, I'm not much of a baseball fan."

Leclerc smiled. "No matter, we've more important things to discuss." He unbuttoned his frock and took out a small pouch and a Bible. He opened the pouch and took out a small loaf of bread, and he handed it to Perry, who in turn hand handed it to the woman.

"Would you please thank her for her hospitality?" Perry said, looking at the priest.

Leclerc smiled and passed along the message. At first, she tried to resist the gift, her proud nature showing through, but a strong look from Perry made her gratefully accept it.

The priest opened the Bible and took out a small map that was folded carefully in the pages. "This is where we are," he said, pointing to a small dot on the map. "And here are the retreating German lines. As you can see, you're about 40 kilometers inside occupied France. With luck, we may be able get you to the front in a few days. We must be extra careful, though. The Germans are in a state of general retreat and are taking and destroying anything and everything at will. At this point, I don't think they would even consider taking prisoners. You would simply be an added burden to them."

Mitchell looked outright scared and Gibbler was uneasy. Perry tried to maintain a positive look, to hide his own fears, knowing that capture now meant almost certain death.

"We must leave now. I will take you to my village where another man will take you to the next town, here." Again the priest pointed to the small map. "It is about 10 kilometers from here."

"Now, in the daylight?" Gibbler asked. "Wouldn't it be safer at night?"

Father Leclerc shook his head. "Any civilians caught traveling at night without specific permission are immediately suspect and taken in for questioning. No, it is better to travel during the day, to hide you in plain sight, so to speak. I will have more food and this time you must not give it away, you will need your strength. We must also get you away from them," he said, looking at the famer and his wife. "If you are caught anywhere near their house, they will be shot on the spot as traitors." Leclerc stood to leave.

"One thing before we go, Father," Perry said. "Would you please tell them how much we appreciate their sacrifice in what they are doing to help us? It's one thing for a soldier to risk his life, but it's something entirely different when you're a civilian and placing yourself in danger for total strangers."

Leclerc smiled and nodded and turned to the old couple and spoke a few words. The woman gestured for the priest to wait as she ran into another room. A few moments later, she returned carrying something wrapped in old newspaper. Gently, she unwrapped it, one fold at a time. As the last piece of paper was folded back, it revealed a picture frame. She took and held the picture to her chest, cradling it like a child, and in a way, it was. It was a photograph of a young man in his late teens in a French Army uniform. She removed the photo and reluctantly handed it to the priest, who in turn handed it to the American airmen.

"This is a photograph of their son, Louis, on his graduation day from the French Military Academy. This was taken shortly before the war. He has been missing since June of 1940 when he was helping the British escape from Dunkirk. They have not heard one word since then, not knowing if he is dead or alive, a prisoner of war or safe in England. You see, René," Leclerc indicated the farmer, "fought against the Germans in the Great War, so they do know something of sacrifice and what they are doing. And no, you are not total strangers, you are allies!"

Perry didn't know what came over him, but at that instant he snapped to attention and saluted the old man and woman and said, "Vive la France! Vive la France!" The old man rose, pulling his shoulders back he stood at attention and returned the salute, sharp as the day when he had worn the uniform nearly thirty years before.

Perry looked at the couple. "I promise you that when we get back to England, I will do everything within my power to find out what happened to your son."

Tears were streaking down the old couple's faces, and before his own tears started to flow, Perry grabbed his men and they went outside. A few moments later, the priest joined them.

"You gave them a wonderful gift today, Captain," Leclerc said. "You have given them the gift of hope, and they haven't had that in a very long time." Perry just shrugged his shoulders, embarrassed by the kind words.

"Come," Leclerc said, "we must hurry!"

CHAPTER ELEVEN

They had found the perfect hiding spot. From an earlier flood, the stream they were following had eroded the bank and several trees had toppled over the embankment, exposing their roots. The underbrush had grown back quickly, hiding the entrance, making it into a root cave and virtually undetectable.

Exhausted, Joe Thomas, Tony Ramos and Jerry Idleman pushed their way through the tangled leaves and branches and crawled into the cave. One big rock protruded from the middle of their little cocoon and they had to skirt around it on their hands and knees.

Once inside, they wearily leaned against the bank, sitting around the rock like it was a campfire. The trio whispered quietly for a few minutes, then fatigue caught up with them and, like hibernating bears, they all drifted off to sleep in their cave.

Thomas awoke with a start. His heart was pounding out a drummer's beat and he was covered in a light sweat; what a nightmare! He sighed as he looked around. It wasn't a nightmare.

"What's going on?" Idleman asked. "You're thrashing around over there like a dog covered in fleas."

"Sorry, bad dream."

"You're telling me," Ramos added as he rolled over. "I wasn't made to sleep on the ground."

"I'm going to have a look around and see if I can find anything to eat," Thomas said. Ramos and Idleman both nodded as they watched their friend crawl toward the entrance.

Watching through the leaves, they could barely see Thomas as he crossed the small stream and scampered up the bank on the other side.

Thomas reached the top of the bank and dusted the dirt off his hands as he stood and looked around. The countryside was beautiful with low rolling hills covered with large stands of trees. Looking back at the stream, he saw several small pools and eddies and bet the fishing must be pretty good here. A pang of homesickness swept through him: he couldn't remember the last time that he had been fishing with his dad and brother. He sighed.

Hearing a dog bark in the distance, Thomas brought himself back to the present. Walking along the trail, he hoped he could find some berries or anything else they could eat. What he really hoped for was to come across a farmhouse with the owners gone so he could go in and discreetly raid the pantry. He continued on the path as it ran along the top of the bank for a few more yards, then followed it as it disappeared into the forest.

Ramos lazily opened one eye. "What'd you say, Jerry?" When Idleman didn't respond, he closed his eye again and tried to go back to sleep. When he heard the voice again, he sat up and was going to chew his friend out for waking him when he looked over and saw that Jerry was still asleep.

Suddenly, the reality of the moment took his breath away. The voice he heard was not that of his friend, but of a stranger... and it was coming from just outside their hiding place. Instantly, he was fully awake and could feel the adrenaline surging through his veins.

Carefully, he reached over and put his hand over Idleman's mouth. Startled, Idleman struggled at first but froze when he saw the intensity burning in Ramos' eyes.

Ramos held his finger to his lips, then tipped his head toward the outside. Peering through the leaves, they could see at least eight German solders milling around in front of their hideaway. As they watched, one soldier bent down and was looking at something in the dirt.

The soldier stood up, and holding a broken branch in his hand, walked over to the officer in charge. He made wide, sweeping motions of the countryside with his hands, then pointed to the opposite side of the stream bank with his finger, stopping at the place where Thomas had climbed up.

The soldier continued to talk to the officer, then turned back around and started pointing to the line of fallen trees where the Americans were hiding. He paused for a moment, staring intently at the trees and slipped his rifle off his shoulder. Instantly the officers started shouting and the other soldiers readied their rifles.

Unsuccessful in his quest for food, Thomas returned along the path. He had just emerged from the trees when he stopped dead in his tracks. From where he was standing, he saw a squad of German soldiers standing to the side of the trees where his friends were hiding. He quickly ducked down behind a nearby log and watched as the Germans took their rifles off their shoulders.

He had to do something, but what? He could take out his pistol and start shooting but he knew he wouldn't stand a chance in a gun battle, and even if he got a couple of them, he'd end up dead or wounded, and Ramos and Idleman would still be in the same predicament. He could slip back into the trees and probably get away but that didn't sit very well with him. But what could he do? Finally he decided to do the only thing he could think of.

He stood up and prepared to run. Hopefully he could lead the soldiers away and give Ramos and Idleman a chance to escape, and if he were lucky, he would get away too. He waited for an incredibly long time, under the circumstances, before one of the soldiers finally looked over and spotted him.

"HALT!"

That was his cue to run. He had just ducked down and turned the corner on the path when he heard the sound of machine guns firing. The log he had just been standing by exploded into splinters. Suddenly this didn't seem like such a good idea anymore.

Ramos and Idleman crouched behind the rock as they watched the deadly drama unfolding before their eyes. Instinctively, they jumped when the German troops started firing at their friend as he scurried over the bank and out of sight. They knew that Thomas was playing rabbit to the foxes so that they could escape. They also knew they had to get out of there and not let his sacrifice be in vain.

Watching intently, as soon as the last soldier had crossed the stream and disappeared into the trees on the far bank, the two darted out of their den and scrambled up the bank behind them. Idleman was in the lead but suddenly stopped at the top of the bank. Ramos was still crawling up the bank, looking back over his shoulder, and ran into Idleman.

"Hey! What'd you stop for?" Ramos said as he reached the top of the bank, then stopped as he answered his own question. A German soldier with his gun over his shoulder was swearing to himself as he was fastening up his pants, running to catch up to his unit. All three froze when they saw each other, looking like grotesque lawn ornaments.

The German was still fumbling with his pants when he finally realized that these were the Americans they were after and his rifle was still slung over his back. Ramos was just one step away and was getting ready to attack when the German decided it would be a good idea to take his gun off his shoulder.

He swung it down so hard and fast he lost his grip. The momentum carried the rifle around and the butt came down and hit Ramos on the side of the head, knocking him off balance. Tripping, Ramos fell to the ground where he hit his head on a rock and was knocked unconscious.

Idleman charged and tackled the soldier. They both went down and Idleman was quick to get back up. He'd done a little wrestling in high school and felt he could take this guy if he stayed in close. He did not want to let him get to his feet and start throwing punches.

He charged in low and grabbed the German by his feet and lifted him up and drove him to the ground hard, putting him down on his back. The German was swinging wildly at Idleman, his arms flailing like a windmill. One of the swings landed a solid blow to the American's ear, and Idleman lost his grip and he rolled away in pain.

The German spun around quickly, holding his ribs with one hand and drew out a bayonet with the other. The bayonet looked like a sword to Idleman as the afternoon sun reflected off the blade. Both men's eyes were filled with terror at the unexpected situation, but the German's held a sign of confidence, now that he had the bayonet.

Idleman tried to draw upon his training, but he had never paid that much attention because as a flyer, he didn't think he would need self-defense because he never planned on getting shot down. He glanced at Ramos lying on the ground. He was stirring slightly but was in no position to help him. Looking at him, he suddenly remembered Ramos telling him about a couple of knife fights he'd been in back in LA when he was growing up. He always thought that Ramos was pulling his leg, but now it seemed to make sense.

Ramos always talked about knowing how the other person handled the knife. Did he swing it and try to cut you by making broad slashes with it, or did he jab with it, trying to stick it in your gut? The only way he could find out was to get close enough for the German to attack him. He didn't much like the prospect of that, but he didn't have a choice. He took a step forward then sidestepped a couple of times. Both times the German lunged forward, trying to stab him.

Okay, now what? What had Ramos said? Why couldn't he remember? With each step and lunge, his adversary was gaining more confidence, becoming a little bolder with each attack. That was it! Ramos had said that when your opponent lunges, step to the side and grab his arm with both hands. At best, if you're lucky, you can get enough leverage and break his arm. At worst, you could dig your fingers into his wrist, hitting the nerve, and make him drop the knife. But he also remembered a warning that Ramos added at the end of the lesson. "Be quick when you grab the arm," he'd said. He'd lifted up his shirt to reveal a three-inch scar along the ribs on his left side.

Idleman slowly circled around, waiting for just the right moment to bait the soldier into making an attack. Any good pilot knows it's best to attack out of the sun, to strike while your enemy can't see, and that's just what this airman from Kentucky did. As soon as the sun was at his back and in the face of the German, he took one step forward and pretended to lunge forward, as if to attack. The German stepped back and lunged forward himself, hoping to catch the American as he moved in.

Idleman was set, ready for the attack with his left foot slightly in front of his right. The German, however, was reacting to Idleman, and moved a little too quickly and was off balance as he charged. As he lunged forward with the knife in his right hand, Idleman leaned out of the path of the blade and grabbed the German's wrist with his right hand, then pulled him forward then latched on with his left. As soon as he had a firm grip with his left hand, he released his right, lifted his elbow and brought it down with all his might on the German's forearm. Idleman heard a howl of pain as the German's hand popped open, dropping the knife to the ground.

Still holding the German's arm, Idleman hit him viciously, as hard as he could, with his free hand. He was rewarded with a loud snap as he broke the soldier's nose. The German retaliated as he lifted his right leg and brought it down, driving the heel of his boot on the top of his attacker's foot.

Idleman recoiled from the pain and released his grip. Both men stumbled apart, falling to the ground. They each spotted the rifle at the same time and the German half crawled, half ran to reach it first. Idleman saw the rifle but he also saw the bayonet.

The German soldier threw himself back onto the ground, lunging for the rifle. He grabbed at it with his left hand and pulled back the bolt with his right as he rolled over with it. But before he could bring it up to fire, Idleman dove on top of him and plunged the blade deep into the center of the German's chest.

Shock and dismay fill both men's eyes as Idleman leaned over the German soldier. He could see and hear him gasping for air, each breath a struggle and getting harder to take than the one before. The soldier's eyes slowly drifted to the bayonet protruding from his chest and then into the eyes of the American hovering over him. The German's eyes were filled with neither terror nor hatred, only disbelief that this had happened to him. He gasped one last breath as his eyes glazed over in death.

Idleman rolled over and sat on the ground, staring into the face of a man he didn't know but had just killed. He didn't know how long he'd been sitting there when he felt a hand on his shoulder.

"You okay?" came the familiar voice of his fellow door gunner.

Idleman didn't move, he just kept staring into the dead man's eyes.

"Come on," Ramos said as he helped Idleman to his feet.

"I-I just murdered this man," Idleman stammered.

Ramos spun him around, putting both hands on his shoulder, looking his distraught friend square in the face. "You did not murder him. This is war and you had to defend yourself. That could easily have been you and me dead over there instead of him. You didn't murder him, you saved my life!"

"I-I guess you're right."

"Of course I am!" Ramos stated loudly. Idleman allowed himself a small smile at Ramos's cockiness.

"Come on, help me drag his body over there and hide it in the bushes. It may buy us a little extra time if they're searching for him and not us." Ramos reached down and grabbed one arm and Idleman reluctantly grabbed the other and started dragging the body. They stuffed it in a hollow behind an oak tree surrounded by low lying bushes. It wasn't the perfect hiding place but it would have to do.

"Okay, let's go. We've got to put as much distance as we can between us and that patrol."

"But what about Joe?"

"He's on his own, he knows that. He made that decision the second he tried to help us out. Now come on." Both men started running deep into the woods, away from the river, away from the soldiers, and away from their friend. They disappeared into the underbrush and never looked back.

CHAPTER TWELVE

Thomas was really having his doubts as to how good an idea this was. Those two knuckleheads had better get away after all this, he thought. He was running hard and fast on a game trail that sliced its way through the forest. He could hear the Germans shouting behind him and it sounded like he was putting a little distance between him and them. He turned to take a quick look and when he turned back around, he ran into a low hanging tree branch. The branch caught him on the left cheek, just below the eye, tearing a large gash in his face and knocking him down.

He lay there, stunned for a moment, then got back up and started running again, then promptly tripped over a tree root and fell down again. The Germans were gaining now and he knew he couldn't outrun them. Deciding to leave the trail, he scampered up a small hill to his right. He climbed about twenty yards, and had just lain down behind a fallen log when he heard the squad of soldiers.

He heard two or three soldiers go running by, then another couple went by at a trot and after a few minutes one or two more went walking by. Thomas refused to let out a sigh of relief; he knew he was far from being out of danger. He decided he would just lie there until after dark, and then follow the original plan and make for the city.

Private Otto Faust staggered along the path and plopped himself down on a tree stump and leaned his rifle on a fallen log. He was exhausted and couldn't move another centimeter. He took off his helmet and pulled a rag from his coat pocket and wiped the perspiration off his forehead.

At 53, he was in no shape to be running around the woods looking for runaway American flyers half his age who could run like a deer. Being overweight didn't help either. At 5'7" and pushing 300 pounds, speed and stamina were not his strong points, and yet, here he was.

Less than a year earlier, October 17th to be exact, a day he would always remember, he was a happy civilian doing his best to survive the war when he received a letter conscripting him into what was called the Volkssturm, the storm of the people, part of the Home Guard. He was told it was his patriotic duty to defend the Fatherland against the invading Allied armies, when in fact he was just one of nearly 250,000 drafted to create new armies to fight in the front lines!

He was given a rifle and an ill-fitting uniform, and the next thing he knew he was fighting in the snow in the middle of the Ardennes Forest against the Americans. At least now, sitting in these woods, he was the hunter instead of the hunted - sort of. He had tried to tell the officer at training camp that he was a pastry chef, not a soldier, but he didn't listen. Because he was fat, they made fun of him and made him their personal servant. Otto get this, Otto get that. It was bad enough being a soldier, but not to be respected as one was even worse.

If only he could capture this American, he would be a hero and they would respect him, but what were the chances of that? He closed his eyes for just a moment, just a moment to relieve the strain. Slowly his head dropped down and relief came as he fell asleep.

Thomas lay there for what he thought was good half hour. He didn't dare move to check his watch. He hadn't heard a sound for a very long time; apparently the soldiers weren't coming back this way. He had been lying on his stomach with his left shoulder pressed against the log and it was beginning to ache. Slowly, carefully, he shifted his weight and moved his arm under him.

Gradually he raised his head above the log and hastily looked around, then quickly ducked back down. He didn't see anything moving, and since no bullets came flying, he decided to get up. With any luck he would find the city, and hopefully run into Ramos and Idleman.

He stood and began brushing the dirt and leaves off his legs when, all of a sudden, out of the corner of his eye he saw him, a German soldier, and he was just sitting there! How could he have been so blind? Because he was sitting still, the soldier's coat had blended perfectly into the dark, wooded background.

He tried to drop back down behind the log, but in his haste, he lost his balance. For one precarious moment, he stood balanced on one foot, teetering between life and death. He swung his arms wildly, like a circus clown performing a high wire act, trying to regain his balance but he lost the struggle and fell headlong over the log, crashing down the hillside sounding like a heard of elk.

Faust's eyes popped open at the thunderous sound. Startled, he stood and grabbed his rifle and spun around just in time to be hit by a flying body. Thomas bounced down the hill and flew off the low embankment, hitting the German at the knees. He knocked the feet out from under the big German and like a mountain falling in an earthquake, the mountain of a man fell right on top of him.

Thomas cringed in pain as his eardrums nearly burst when the rifle went off just a few feet from his head. Then he felt himself being crushed as the big German landed on top of him, his massive weight driving the air from his lungs. He had cuts and bruises from his fall down the hillside, but none of that mattered now, he couldn't breathe! He gasped for breath, but none would come, his lungs couldn't draw a breath with the weight of the German on him.

He began flailing his arms and legs wildly, trying to move the mountain, but the German was unmovable. Slowly he began to grow faint and he was beginning to see spots and his vision was growing red. Thomas was on the verge of panic and he knew it. His head was exploding from the pressure and yet he continued to struggle, and in the whirlwind of thoughts racing through his head, he was proud of the fact that he didn't give in to blind panic and that he had kept his head.

As he was struggling, a strange thought flashed across his fading mind; he knew that when he had joined the service he had a very real chance of dying. He knew he could die by going down with the plane, being hit by flak or enemy fighters, but never in a million years would he have thought that he would die in Germany, crushed to death by a fat soldier. He took one last desperate gasp for air, and when none reached his lungs, he felt his eyes roll back in his head and then he was gone.

The rifle went off when the American came tumbling down the hillside and hit him in the legs. In a near panic,

Faust struggled to get up, but each time his hands were knocked out from under him by the flyer who was swinging his arms about wildly.

Faust was scared. He was not a professional soldier who didn't know how to fight and besides, this young American was at least half his age. He snapped his head back and forth, eyes darted around the ground, where was his rifle? At last he spotted it, but it had landed a good two meters away. If he got up, the American might reach it first, and then what would he do? Surely the American would kill him.

Suddenly, he realized that the American's thrashing was getting weaker. He also noticed that he was struggling to breathe, that each breath was a long, loud gasp. Then it dawned on him: the American couldn't get up! And on top of that, he couldn't breathe! Finally the American stopped moving altogether.

Faust waited for a moment, then rolled off and crawled on his hands and knees as fast as he could and grabbed his rifle. He spun around and sat down fumbling with the bolt, trying to get the old shell out and chamber a new cartridge. His hands were shaking so badly he couldn't get the action to work. Finally the old round kicked out and he got a new cartridge in then brought the barrel of the rifle up and pointed it at the American lying deathly still on the ground. Faust was having a hard time keeping a steady aim because his chest was heaving with each breath.

Gradually his heart and breathing steadied, and he struggled to one knee, then up to both feet. Rifle still at the ready, Faust slowly walked over to the still body. Was he dead? Did he kill him? His stomach turned at the very thought that he had taken another human being's life, but what else could he have done?

Just then, two men burst through the bushes; startled, Faust spun around and trained his rifle on them. They looked at the German, then at the American lying at his feet, then back at the German.

"Otto? Did you capture the American?" It was Sergeant Bauer asking the question. Bauer had been one of his cruelest tormentors. A flash of inspiration ignited in Faust's brain; this was his chance. Yes, he had captured him, but not how they were thinking. What was he to say, "Yes, I caught him... by sitting on him." Most important was that he had captured the American flyer, not how he did it.

Faust lowered his weapon then sat down on a tree stump and tipped his helmet back. "It was a terrible struggle," he began with a grave look on his face. "He came charging at me, running down the hill like a wild animal. He tackled me, hitting me at my knees, sending us both into the dirt. I sprang to my feet and we circled each other like prizefighters. We traded a few punches, if you want to call his hits punches," he said, smiling, trying to make it sound like he fought all the time.

"The foolish American grew impatient and charged me like an old ram. I sidestepped his attack and got him in a headlock and choked him into submission. He lies where he fell," Faust said with a triumphant smile, then kicked the American once, reinforcing the point that he was the victor. Suddenly, the still body of the American jerked as he drew a loud and long gasp.

"You didn't kill him?" the sergeant asked.

Faust was a little startled that American wasn't dead, but then quickly recovered. "No, I wanted him alive. He might have valuable information that we can use."

By now, the rest of the squad had returned and they were all standing around, looking at the American, who was lying on the ground coughing. "How did you catch him, Sergeant?" one of the soldiers asked.

"I didn't," Bauer replied, "Private Faust did." In unison the entire squad looked at Faust. At first their eyes were full of disbelief but then they slowly filled with admiration, then something Faust had been longing for most—respect.

"Private Faust," Lieutenant Schubert, the officer in charge, said, "if you will take your prisoner, we will head back to the river."

Faust nodded smartly then grabbed the flyer by the back of his coat and dragged him to his feet. The American got to one knee, then stood on shaky legs, holding his ribs. Faust pushed him down the trail with the rest of the squad following. Private Otto Faust was in his moment of glory, in the front of the procession as he led them back to the river.

Thomas tried to keep pace, but staggered every time the big German pushed him, trying to make him go faster. His ribs were sore and he was sure one or two were cracked, and he was cut and bruised all over from his fall down the hillside. Each step was a growing agony as his left knee and ankle began to swell. He needed to rest but he knew he dare not stop.

Apprehension mounted with every step down the trail. He didn't remember it being this long and it seemed to stretch forever. He wondered if at the other end he would find Ramos and Idleman sitting tied up by the bank or if they had managed to get away. The sound of the river grew louder until they broke free of the trail and were standing on the bank.

He paused at the top of the bank, relieved to look across the stream and see that Ramos and Idleman weren't there. He should have known better than to stop because the very next instant, he felt a boot in the small of his back as it kicked him over the edge and down the embankment. The pain was tremendous as he ended in a twisted heap at the bottom. Every muscle cried out in pain but he refused to utter a sound. He was bound and determined not to give them the satisfaction of hearing him cry out.

He struggled to his feet, then began to cross the steam. The water felt good, its coldness numbing some of his hurt. As they reached the other side, several of the soldiers started to call out to someone. Thomas didn't know who it was nor did he care. He climbed up the embankment where they allowed him to sit down.

As he lowered himself onto a log, he realized how good it felt to be able just to sit and rest. As bad as it sounded, he hoped the prison camp was nearby. While the other soldiers spread out and started searching for their comrade, the fat German sat down beside him.

He leaned his rifle against the log, then took out a handkerchief and casually wiped the sweat from his forehead. He glanced over at the American staring at him and suddenly thought it would be a good idea to keep his rifle trained on him. Faust tried to look tough as he put his handkerchief away then picked up his rifle and laid it across his lap, pointing it at his prisoner.

Suddenly one of the soldiers started shouting: "Snell, snell! Hurry hurry, Lieutenant, come here!" The young soldier was standing next to a large tree, looking pale and very frightened. The rest of the squad hurried over to see what he had found. The lieutenant pushed his way through the men and paused when he saw what they were staring at.

"It's Hirsch," one of them muttered.

Lieutenant Schubert kneeled down and pulled away the branches that had been hastily thrown over the body. The soldier's chest was covered with blood and one of the young soldiers in the squad quickly turned away and vomited, having never seen death before.

"The other American flyers must have done this," Schubert said. His words were slow and deliberate, hate growing with each syllable. "This one led us away so his friends could kill Hirsch and escape."

For a brief moment, the lieutenant just stared at the blood-soaked tunic of his soldier, then in the blink of an eye, he shot up like a rocket. His men parted as he cut through them like the bow of a mighty ship. With long, purposeful, angry strides, Schubert set his course toward their prisoner. Without breaking stride, he reached down and unsnapped his holster and drew out his pistol.

When he was ten feet away, he stopped abruptly and aimed at the American's head. Thomas started to turn to see what was going on, but never got that far. He never even heard the gun go off, much less feel the bullet as it entered his right temple. He was dead before his body hit the dirt with a dull thud.

Faust was sitting right behind Thomas when he was shot. Stunned, he looked down at the front of his uniform and saw that it was speckled with blood and brain matter. He was numb as he stared down at the dead American, who a moment ago had been his prize.

"Look what they did to Hirsch!" Schubert shouted, pointing back at their fallen comrade. "We will not allow the American swine to get away with this. We will track them down and punish them. They will pay for their crime!"

Not a word was spoken, nor did any of the soldiers move. They were as still as the dead bodies in front of them. "Night is about to fall and we won't be able to track the Americans in the dark. We will take our fallen brother home and return in the morning to hunt the Americans down!"

CHAPTER THIRTEEN

They pulled into the barn behind the church of the priest's village. Perry and the others stood and stretched as they looked at their next ride to freedom.

"Not exactly Cinderella's coach, is it, sir?" Mitchell said.

Perry chuckled. "No, but as long as it gets us out of here, I don't care."

Their next ride was a rickety looking wagon filled with hay. Harnessed to it was an old mare that had been put out to pasture many years ago. The horse was so old and sway-backed, she looked like she should be giving children rides at a county fair instead of working and pulling a cart. The driver was a short man of about 40, with the same leathery complexion as the farmer. He wore dirty overalls and a large floppy brimmed straw hat. Both he and the horse looked tired.

Perry walked up to the man and held out his hand. "Hi, I'm Captain Mike..."

"Please, monsieur, no names," he said with a heavy accent. "The less I know, the safer we all are. For now, you can call me Claude."

"I understand," Perry answered.

"You and your men get in the wagon and lie as close to the sides as you can. Put the boy up front, right behind my seat." Mitchell grunted at being called a boy. It was bad enough being called that at home, but to have a foreigner call him that made it all the worse.

"It will be a long, hot, and uncomfortable journey for you, but this is the quickest and safest way to get you back to your lines," the driver said. "There is a little food for the trip and I will share it with you along the way. When we come to a checkpoint, remain absolutely still and don't make a sound. Do you all understand?"

All three Americans nodded. They each shook hands with the priest and thanked him for all his help, then turned and crawled into the back of the wagon, burrowing into the hay like mice eating their way into a block of cheese. With a jerk, the wagon stared moving and they were on their way.

After an hour of nothing but the monotonous sound of the horse's hooves plodding on the dirt road, they heard the distant sound of voices. "We are coming to a small village, be very still and quiet," Claude said. "There are still German sympathizers here who would think nothing of turning you over to the Gestapo."

As they entered the village, it was like listening to a radio program back home, Perry thought. He could hear everything that was going on but couldn't see anything. It was a great temptation to pull away the hay so he could see, but a temptation he knew could be fatal if they were caught. The dull, soft plodding of the horse's hooves on the country road had been replaced with a clippity-clop as they moved from the dirt to the cobblestone streets.

The pace of life sounded relaxed and slow as they rode through the town. He could hear other horse-drawn carts going down the streets and the constant sound of bicycle bells jingling. He also heard the occasional sound of a car passing by and the deeper rumble of truck engines, which scared him the most, since the military were the only ones running vehicles like that out here in the country.

Once he thought he heard the sound of a tank clanking down one of the back streets, but he couldn't be sure. More than anything he wanted to look, but the fear of death kept him from peering out.

But most interesting of all were the sounds of the people. As a kid, he would lie on his parents' floor in the front room and they would huddle around the radio listening to programs like The Lone Ranger, Dick Tracey, and Amos and Andy, and the music of the big bands.

He would listen to the programs, hearing all the sounds and imagine what the people looked like and what was happening. If it weren't for the fact that he was afraid for his life and the lives of his men, he would have actually enjoyed the ride and listening to everything.

Fortunately, they weren't stopped, and soon it turned quiet as they were alone again on the country road. They had been traveling for about two hours, dozing in and out from the boredom, when they heard the distant sounds of aircraft engines.

Even from 20,000 feet, there was no mistaking the sounds of the B-17 engines. The drone of the formation of flying fortresses was like getting a letter from home, both comforting and reassuring. It was a large formation, at least 500 planes, Perry guessed, and if he listened carefully enough, he could occasionally hear the higher pitched whine of the escorts. But above all, the sound of nearly 2,000 bomber engines singing in unison was truly music to his ears.

Suddenly, he could hear the melody beginning to sour. A new and different sound was blending in, creating a strange and terrible harmony—enemy fighters! They were too far away to hear the individual sound of machine gun fire, but he knew what was going to happen; he had lived it 19 times.

With chilling reality, he could imagine the scene unfolding. He could see the bombers tightening up their formation as the enemy fighters engaged. He could hear the chatter over the intercoms, the gunners calling out bandits, coming in low, high, setting up for another attack. He could see the silver winged mustangs swooping down on the attacking fighters like guardian angels.

Smoke would be filling the blue sky now, creating its own cloud, turning it a hazy gray. Trails of smoke from damaged engines, smoke from planes that were on fire and smoke from planes that had exploded, both friend and foe.

The air would also be filled with falling planes and falling men. Parachutes would flood the sky, floating down like lazy snowflakes on a calm winter's day. Perry squeezed his eyes tight, breaking the all too real images that had been burned into his mind.

Suddenly there was a tremendous noise. The crashing of metal as it twisted and snapped upon hitting the earth and the sizzling and crackling sound of fire burning uncontrollably.

The cart jolted as the startled old horse began running with amazing speed. The three passengers bounced up and down and were tossed around the wagon as Claude struggled to regain control over the frightened animal. Perry could hear him yelling at the horse and didn't need any translator to know that the Frenchman was swearing at her, trying to get her to slow down.

"What's going on?" Perry asked.

"Quiet, monsieur, there are Germans soldiers coming. One of your bombers has crashed and the crew is parachuting down and the Germans are capturing them."

"Can we help them?"

"No, we will be lucky if we don't get caught ourselves. Now please, remain quiet."

Claude finally regained control over the frightened animal and they returned to their plodding speed. Just then Perry heard the sounds of several trucks rushing up from the rear. Two roared past and then a third sped by, but it skidded to a stop in front of them and he heard shouting. He was jolted by the sound of machine gun fire and more shouting.

Perry held his breath and could hear a German solider walking from the truck. Now he stood right beside the cart, shouting at Claude. Claude was talking to the soldier and remained in his seat until Perry heard the sound of the bolt being pulled back on a rife. At that, Claude had no choice but to get down.

The Frenchman gave the soldier his identification papers and work pass and continued talking, hoping to distract him. The soldier didn't trust him as he circled the wagon, inspecting it and accusing him of smuggling airmen.

Claude just laughed, pointing out that he had been on the road the entire time and that they had even seen him on the road when the parachutes were falling. Finally, Claude went to the front of the wagon, hopped back up on the seat and reached for a pitchfork lying across the hay.

The guard shouted, "Halt!" and raised his gun. Claude smiled as he took the pitchfork and carefully aimed it, jabbing it several times into the middle of the hay pile, trying to convince the soldier that he didn't have anyone hiding in his wagon. He just hoped the Americans had listened to him and were lying near the sides.

Claude jabbed twice more, hitting the floor, making the point that the wagon was empty. He then smiled and attempted to hand the pitchfork to the guard so he could see for himself, but the solider refused, and seemed satisfied that there were no stowaways hidden in the hay.

The soldier dismissed him and Claude climbed back up onto his seat. They had traveled about thirty or forty yards, and Perry and the others were just beginning to sigh with relief when they heard the soldier shout "HALT!" and a single gunshot echoed out.

Claude pulled back on the reins so hard and fast he thought he'd broken the horse's neck. He held his breath and slowly raised his hands and turned around. With relief, Claude saw that the soldier was facing the other direction and was shouting at an airman who had parachuted down at the edge of the field. Claude quickly turned back around and started the wagon again.

It was late afternoon now and the sun was full and hot. The air was stifling and stale under the hay and Perry and his men were getting stiff and sore from the hours of bouncing around in the back of the wagon, but their French guide refused to stop. He told them he didn't want to take the chance of being spotted and said they would be stopping shortly for the night.

The three stowaways groaned softy but knew there was nothing they could do, and that Claude was right. After all, they were fighting for their lives, not going on a sightseeing trip. Claude handed down a small bottle of wine and a half loaf of bread to his passengers. Each man took his share and passed it along to the next. The wine had a vinegar taste to it and the bread was stale, but they didn't care. Within moments, the bottle was empty and the bread was gone.

The sun was starting to set when they turned off the main road and Claude told them they were at their destination for the night. The cart soon pulled into a courtyard that didn't look that different from the one they had left that morning. The barn door was open and they drove straight in. Claude got down and closed the barn door, then told the Americans they could come out.

Slowly the men poked their heads out of the hay, like kids ending a game of hide and seek. Each in turn crawled out of the wagon and stood and stretched, looking at his new surroundings.

Perry took his jacket off and shook out the straw. As a kid, he would spend the summers at his uncle's farm and buck hay for a little money to go see the Saturday matinees. He always enjoyed the wagon ride back to the barn from the fields, sitting on top of the hay, but after this, it would be the last time he would ever want to take another hay ride.

A tall man in his mid-forties was talking to Claude. He was dressed in black pants and black sweater with a dark green beret. He looks so French, Perry thought, then laughed at himself for such a stupid thought, since he was French and they were in the middle of France. They exchanged the usual greetings, giving a kiss on either cheek, something Perry could still not get used to. When they finished talking, the man turned and approached Perry, who quickly stuck out his hand.

"I'm Cap…" Perry hesitated at his name, remembering what the priest and "Claude" had told them about names and being captured, "…happy to meet you."

The Frenchman smiled. "Yes, Captain Perry, we're aware of who you and your crew are, and we'll leave it at that for the introductions. You may call me Franc."

Perry nodded his head. "Yes, I understand."

"We were hoping to smuggle you and your men out tomorrow night, but there has been a change of plans."

CHAPTER FOURTEEN

Ramos and Idleman rushed headlong down the path, driven more by blind fear than by thoughts of capture. Ramos threw his arm up to push a tree branch back then let it go behind him. Idleman didn't see the branch as it whipped back and caught him in the face. He let out a yelp of pain as it raked him across his left cheek. Idleman stumbled to his knees as he grabbed his face, blood trickling between his fingers as he grasped at the open wound.

"I'm sorry, man," Ramos said as he rushed back to help his friend. "I thought you were watching." Ramos took out a handkerchief and began treating the wound. He slowly pried away Idleman's fingers and wiped away the blood. "This isn't too bad," he said. There were four slash marks across his face, only one of which was deep. "When you get back home, you can tell all the ladies that you were in a sword fight with a German officer or something."

"More like with his cat," Idleman replied. They both smiled, but it was fleeting as a single shot rang out and echoed in the distance.

"Do you suppose..."

"Nah," Idleman quickly cut him off.

"Yeah, you're right. Let's get out of here." Neither wanted to think that the shot could have meant that their friend had been killed. Ramos stood, then reached down and helped his friend to stand.

Idleman got to his feet, wiped his face, then looked at the blood on the handkerchief.

"Not too bad, huh? I wonder if you'd say that if this was your blood instead of mine?"

Ramos smiled. "If I told you what it really looks like, you'd faint dead away. Now come on."

Idleman frowned, then followed his fellow gunner.

After an hour of silent walking, Idleman spoke. "Evening falls pretty quickly in the forest, it's not dark yet but we should be keeping an eye out for a good place to spend the night."

Ramos shook his head. "I want to get to the city as soon as possible. I hate this country stuff." He flicked a leaf as he walked by. "I was meant to be surrounded by tall buildings, not tall trees, and to have pavement under my feet, not dirt."

"Didn't you ever go to camp or anything as a kid?"

"Nah, the closest thing we had to that was a vacant lot two blocks down. I love the sounds of the city, the cars going by, the trollies, all the people. It's too quiet out here. I prefer the honking of a car to the chirping of a bird."

Idleman shook his head. "I grew up in a small lumber town where the outdoors was just part of life. We'd go camping and fishing and spend hours playing in the woods. I guess I got into the big city as often as you got into the country, so none of this bothers me like it does you."

"I just know that I'll feel much safer once we're in the city."

Idleman just shrugged his shoulders and continued walking.

It was late afternoon when the pair of runaway B-17 gunners collapsed a few yards off the trail. Both were tired and hungry and needed to rest. Idleman collapsed with his back against a tree, his knees pulled tightly into his chest.

Mindlessly, he rocked slowly back and forth. He just couldn't believe that in less than 24 hours, he had been shot down, separated from the rest the crew, almost captured and had KILLED a man face to face. It was almost more than the country boy from Kentucky could handle.

Ramos wanted to curl up in a ball in the tall ferns and sleep, hoping things would be different, that he could wake up from this nightmare, but the streetwise kid from L.A. knew better. All his life he'd seen trouble and been in numerous fights, but this was different, much different. This wasn't for some stupid control of turf or who owned the block stuff. This was as real as it got, and for once in his life he was scared, really scared. If he hadn't been raised the way he had, he knew he would have lost it a long time ago. He went to sleep wondering at and admiring how his country bumpkin partner could handle it.

Idleman awoke with a start. He didn't know if he had had a nightmare but he was fully awake now. He looked at his watch; they had been asleep for only an hour. He looked at the lowering sun then went over and woke his companion. "Come on, Tony, I figure we've got about seven or eight miles to go."

"Good," Ramos replied as he pulled a twig out of his hair.

"I'm no Daniel Boone, but I think we should stay to the high ground here and follow the ridge as far as we can. Once we get in sight of the city, we'll hide until dark and you can take us from there."

Ramos agreed and the pair began walking west. They talked a little on their journey, but mostly they traveled in silence. Both were careful not to bring up what might have happened to their friend.

CHAPTER FIFTEEN

"You're a very lucky man, Sergeant," the man said as he took Billy Jacobs into the cabin. "You will be picked up tonight and taken to a safe house, and from there delivered to another cell that will take you safely across the German lines into free France. From there you will be able to contact your own army and return to England."

"Thank you, mister...?" Jacobs said.

"It is better if you don't know my name, just in case you're captured, but for now, you may call me Florus."

Jacobs nodded. He had no intention of getting captured, but he did understand. He was awfully glad he lived in the States; these people in Europe sure did some mighty strange things. He didn't want to live in a place where they gave girl's names to boys or where they'd drop everything they were doing just to have some tea. Nope, he couldn't wait to get back home to Shreveport, Louisiana, where things were normal.

Florus continued, "In about an hour, a car will pick you up. There may be one or two others in the car. They are Allied soldiers as well, but again, for security measures, you should not talk to each other until you get to your safe house. Don't panic if you come to armed checkpoints. We have bribed the guards so you should have no trouble."

Again, Jacobs just nodded his head.

"You'll find some bread in the pantry and a bottle of wine next to it. Help yourself, then try to get some rest. The next few days will be trying ones."

"Thank you," Jacobs said and disappeared into the kitchen. He found everything just as Florus had said, and after he had his fill, he returned to the living room and waited in a wooden chair that had a worn and tattered pad that had long since gone flat.

It was the warmest and most comfortable chair he'd sat in in a long time and sleep overtook him before he even knew it was coming. Just as suddenly, he felt a hand on his shoulder. Even though he was exhausted, he woke up instantly.

"The car is here," Florus said, "it is time to go. The driver's name is Jacques, but remember, no talking."

Jacobs held out his hand. "Thank you, Florus, I really appreciate all your help, and if you are ever in Shreveport, be sure to look me up. I'd love to repay your hospitality."

Florus shook his hand, then opened the front door. Jacobs stepped down from the porch and opened the car door and quietly got in. There were two men in the back seat, one wearing an airman's uniform like his and the other regulation army combat fatigues. All three looked at each other with suspicion and no one said a word as Jacob's got in and shut the door.

The car started rolling and Jacobs casually looked at his two companions. Could either of these guys really be a spy? If they were, they were sure well prepared. Both had on the right clothes and were dirty and yes, the soldier he was sitting next to reeked.

"How long you boys been on the run?" Jacobs asked indifferently. At first, neither one said a word, then finally the airman spoke. He was a P-47 jug pilot and had been shot down four days ago while strafing an airfield south of here. This seemed to ease the tension a little and the foot soldier explained how he had been separated from his unit, captured once, escaped, then got caught again.

They spoke briefly but the conversation soon died as no one really trusted the others. With nothing else to do, Jacobs laid his head against the window and went to sleep.

It seemed like he had been asleep only a short time when he felt the car slowing to a stop. "What's going on?" Jacobs asked. The driver got out of the car without saying a word and went to the trunk. All three soldiers piled nervously out of the car.

"Here," Jacques said, throwing a bundle of clothes to each one. "Put these on. We are coming to a checkpoint soon and I can't be seen hauling around a bunch of Allied soldiers."

"But in civilian clothes, won't the German take us for spies if we're caught and shoot us?" Jacobs asked.

"Maybe, but you'll be caught for sure wearing American uniforms. I don't have time to argue. If you want to come with me, then change now; if not, then you can leave. It makes no difference to me."

Jacobs didn't like the driver's tone of voice, and he didn't like being told what to do by a stranger but he knew he didn't have much choice. Reluctantly, all three changed and the driver took their uniforms and hid them in a secret compartment in the trunk.

Without another word, they got back in and continued. He hated having to depend on other people. He was used to taking care of himself. Even when he was a boy, both parents would be gone all day at work and he would be home alone to fend for himself after school.

But now he was depended on strangers in a strange land to keep him safe and it didn't sit well with him. For the next few minutes he continued to worry, trying to decide if he should stay in the car or take his chances, when suddenly the question was answered for him.

Jacobs sat up straight as he looked out the front windshield and saw a checkpoint with half a dozen German soldiers milling around. "Okay, everyone just sit quietly and don't say a word," the driver ordered. "Don't panic and we'll be fine. Everything has been taken care of."

Jacobs nervously pretended to be asleep, but peered through his eyelids, keeping a close watch on everything. The car pulled to a stop in front of the single barricade that hung across the road. One guard approached the driver's window while two other guards sat on a wooden crate smoking. No one seemed too concerned about their presence, as a third guard appeared from behind some bushes redoing his belt, obviously having just relieved himself.

The guard asked for the driver's papers, then eyed the three men in the back seat. He stepped back and glanced through the papers, handing them back and motioned for them to continue on. Passing through the checkpoint, the driver looked back and reassured them that everything was fine, to relax and that they would be at their destination soon.

The other two passengers looked relived, but Jacobs was not so reassured. True, Florus had said the guards were bribed and that there would be no trouble, and there wasn't, but something in the back of his mind was saying he wasn't out of the woods yet. He now sat up and paid closer attention to the surroundings and to what was going on. They were definitely heading toward they city and out of the country, which he didn't like all that much.

It made sense though, that there would be more resistance contacts in the city and what better place to hide than in plain sight, but still... Jacobs couldn't believe that his two companions had drifted off to sleep, what was the matter with them? Was he just being paranoid? Losing his nerve?

The car was now on the outskirts of a small city. They drove past the rail yards that had been bombed, along with other portions of the city. Even in the dark, he could see that the devastation caused by air raids was tremendous and horrific. It bothered him a little to think that he might be responsible for some of this, but reminded himself that he didn't start this war.

The streets were dark and empty, a blackout in place because of the raids. They passed by several military trucks going in the opposite direction and a couple of squads of soldiers marching to somewhere in a hurry.

Jacobs also noticed that the driver kept looking in the mirror at them. Was he getting nervous for some reason?

"Relax, Sergeant, we'll soon be there," Jacques said, noticing Jacobs staring at him.

There was a tone in the drive's voice that Jacobs thought was odd and a little unsettling. The car turned a corner onto the main thoroughfare, and up ahead Jacobs caught a glimpse of a Nazi flag hanging in front of one of the buildings. His heart started pounding and he looked at the driver who had a huge smirk on his face. They had been betrayed!

Jacobs shook the two sleeping men and shouted that it was a trap. Jacobs saw the driver reach in his coat and his first thought was he was going for a gun. He looked out the window and judged that they were going about 20mph. Without a second thought, he threw the car door open and jumped out. He hit the cobblestones hard, and rolled awkwardly over and over until he slammed into the curb.

He felt a sharp pain in his left wrist as he hit the curb; he only hoped that it wasn't broken. The car skidded to a halt and the driver jumped out, gun in hand. Jacobs sprang to his feet and started running. A shot rang out, sounding like a howitzer in the still of the night, and the "artillery round" landed wide, chipping a big chunk out of the sidewalk five feet to his left. Jacobs glanced over his shoulder to see that the infantryman had kicked open the back door, hitting the driver and sending him sprawling into the street.

Jacobs darted down an alleyway and heard more shouting and then another gunshot. He silently thanked the soldier for giving him the time to escape and said a quick prayer for him. He stumbled as he ran around a corner, slipping on the wet cobblestones, landing hard on his left side. He tried to protect his wrist as best he could, but the sudden jolt of hitting the ground again sent a surge of pain that nearly made him pass out.

He heard the squeal of truck tires stopping and then the shouting of troops as they jumped down; he knew he had to keep moving. Getting up as quickly as his battered body would allow, he raced on down the alleyway. The shouts were getting louder, they were gaining on him; he knew he had to get off the streets. Desperately, he tried a door on his right, but it was locked. He tried another and then another with the same results. He could feel frustration and hopelessness grabbing him by the throat, making it hard to breathe. The sound of the pounding boots of the approaching soldiers echoed through the narrow alleyway, sounding like an entire division was descending upon him. There was one door left. If he couldn't get it open, he knew he was done for.

He grabbed for the door handle but his trembling hand slipped off. He reached for it again, using both hands this time and there was a loud click and the door flew open. He jumped inside and slammed it shut, quickly locking it. Jacobs threw his back against the door as his eyes darted back and forth in the dark room trying to make out where he was. He tried to listen but found it impossible over the rushing sound of his heaving chest and the blood pounding in his ears as he gasped for breath.

The sound of pounding boots rushed passed the door and he let out a small sigh of relief; he had escaped... for the moment. He froze in terror as he heard someone rattling the door handle. He held his breath and braced himself in case they tried to break it down. After an eternity, he heard the solitarily footsteps move on to the next door.

His eyes grew accustomed to the dark and he began to make out shapes. He was in some sort of storage room full of large crates and barrels; this would make a good place to hide, he thought as he eased along the wall and nestled himself between two stacks of crates. He would wait for several hours then slip out and hopefully make his escape back into the country.

Jacobs drew a deep breath as he leaned against one of the crates. At last he had a moment to relax and he wondered what had happened to the airman and the soldier. How could they have been betrayed? Was it the farmer? Did he sell him out for food or for some other reason? Was it Florus? Was he working for the Gestapo, or was the driver just doing it on his own to earn a few francs? He would find out and come back after the war to show that snake-in-the-grass a little Southern style justice, the way they do it back home.

He suddenly realized just how exhausted he was and it was becoming a struggle to keep his eyelids open. He shifted position to get a little more comfortable and before he knew it, he was asleep. But slumber didn't last as he awoke to a loud commotion just outside the storage room door leading to the inside of the building.

He heard shouting and then the sound of something hitting the floor followed by the sound of footsteps, lots of footsteps. The Germans were going door to door searching for him.

He thought about making a break for it but he knew there were probably several guards outside in the alley and if he came rushing out, they'd probably shoot first and ask questions later. If he were lucky, he might be able to hide himself well enough and they wouldn't find him. He moved around the corner and pulled several empty boxes around him and prayed his luck would continue to hold. He had just finished when the door burst open.

Peering through the cracks in the crates he counted at least five soldiers, all carrying machine pistols. One soldier walked right past him on his way to check the back door. Jacobs could see the caked mud on his boots and a long, red scuff mark on the side that it looked like he had rubbed or kicked the leather against something. Jacobs became sick to his stomach; was it blood?

The soldier rattled the door to make sure it was locked and then turned around and started walking back. Suddenly the soldier stopped and so did Jacobs' heart. He held his breath, willing with all his might that the soldier would keep on walking, but he didn't.

The soldier started shouting and throwing the boxes aside. He was quickly joined by two others and within a matter of moments the country boy from Louisiana was staring down the barrels of three German machine pistols.

Jacobs held up his hands in surrender but the soldiers continued to shout. One reached down and grabbed him by the wrist and yanked him to his feet. Jacobs let out a scream of pain as the soldier grabbed his injured wrist. The sudden scream made them even more nervous and they knocked Jacobs back down and started kicking him, trying to beat the resistance out of him.

Jacobs tried to raise his hands again and kept shouting that he surrendered, but the soldiers would have none of it. They kept hitting and kicking him, taking their own frustrations out on this lone American airman. After a few minutes, the officer who had been standing at the door walked over and ordered his men to stop.

Jacobs lay on the floor, curled in a ball and gasping for breath. He had managed to protect himself from most of the blows, but a few had gotten through and he was bleeding from his mouth and nose, and he could add a cracked rib or two to his injured wrist.

The German captain looked down at him with a disinterested look and asked, "Can you walk?" Jacobs nodded and struggled to his feet. The soldiers quickly surrounded him and shoved him out into the street. There was a large troop truck sitting in the street, and parked right behind it was the car he had ridden in. Leaning against it, smoking a cigarette, was the driver. He smirked as he saw Jacobs being led out.

Jacobs felt an instant, burning rage when he saw the man who had betrayed him and the smirk just made it worse. Jacobs stared at him as they passed each other. With a quickness that surprised everyone, Jacobs lashed out with a single, tremendous swing with his right fist.

The blow was accurate and delivered with the fury of revenge. Jacobs' fist landed squarely on the driver's nose and Jacobs was rewarded for his effort by the sound of breaking cartilage and bone. His momentum carried forward and they both slammed into the car, but before he could hit him again, Jacobs felt the strong hands of the soldiers grabbing him.

The driver stood there holding his nose and screaming. Jacobs couldn't understand what he was saying but he had a pretty good idea that he was using every swear word in the French vocabulary; now it was his turn to smirk.

The driver looked at his blood-covered hands and then at Jacobs. He swore again and started to move toward him. Jacobs prepared himself though there was not much he could do, being held by the two soldiers. The driver swung and sunk his big fist into Jacobs' stomach, and the flyer doubled over in pain, followed by a left jab to the side, causing even more pain in his cracked ribs. The Frenchman continued with a quick upper cut, hitting Jacobs in the jaw, snapping his head back.

The driver stepped back and wiped the blood from his face. He looked at his hand and then smiled sadistically at Jacobs. "Now I'm going to break your nose." The driver stepped up and was about to hit Jacobs when a hand across his chest held him back. The German officer looked at him and spoke a few words. The driver started to protest but he was cut short by a shout from the German as two more soldiers stepped up.

The driver sneered at Jacobs but held up his hands in surrender, backing away. All Jacobs could manage to do was to raise his head and give a brief nod of gratitude to the captain. They threw him like a bag of dirt into the truck. Jacobs let out a yelp before he passed out from the pain.

CHAPTER SIXTEEN

Billy Jacobs woke up looking at the sun. It was big, bright, and felt warm against his face, but something didn't seem right. Slowly his eyes focused and he recognized that it wasn't the sun but a bright light bulb. Gaining more of his senses, he realized that he was sitting in a chair in a small, nondescript room in front of an equally plain looking desk.

He reached down and gently touched his tender ribs. They had been tightly wrapped, and though still sore, the wrappings made his breathing a lot easier. He was just about to get up when he heard the door open. A major, wearing the lightning SS on his collar, walked in carrying a thin manila file folder.

"I am Major Vogler," he said as he sat down at the desk, folding his hands over the folder. "You've be through quite an ordeal Sergeant. Tell me something, was it worth it?"

Jacobs didn't understand the question and the look on his face reflected that.

"Hitting the driver, I mean. Was it worth the beating that you took for it?"

"Did I break his nose?"

Vogler nodded. "Yes."

Jacobs smiled with satisfaction. "If I broke his nose, then yes sir, it was."

The major smiled back. "I like you, Sergeant. I have just a few questions for you. If you answer them honestly and quickly, your stay here will be short and pleasant. Otherwise, I will be forced to employ methods I would rather not use in order to get the information I need. The choice is entirely up to you."

"My name is Jacobs, William H., serial number 6335148."

Vogler shook his head. "Come now, Billy... that is what your friends call you, isn't it? Billy? You can do better than that."

"Jacobs, William H., 6335148."

Vogler sighed. "I was hoping we could do this the civilized way." Vogler opened the folder and started reciting from it without even looking at its contents.

"William, or Billy, Henry Jacobs, born December 24, 1924 at County General Hospital in Shreveport, Louisiana. You are, or should I say were, the tail gunner in B-17G serial number 232102, also known as the *Red Light Lady*, piloted by Captain Michael Perry." Vogler closed the file then stood and walked slowly behind Jacobs.

"I could go on, but what's the point? That Billy Jacobs that I spoke about is not here. There is no one in this room wearing an American uniform. I only see a man wearing civilian clothes, and since I don't see a military uniform, I can only assume that the man sitting in front of me is a spy, and as you know, we have every right to shoot spies, no questions asked."

"I'm no spy!" Jacobs said, anxiety filling his voice.

Vogler grabbed the back of Jacob's chair, then spun him around quickly. "Then prove it!" He shouted in his face. "Tell me something to convince me that you are the man in that folder and not a spy to be shot."

Jacobs swallowed hard and answered, "Jacobs, William H..."

"Is not in this room!" Vogler shouted, slamming his hands onto the table "I see only a spy who will be executed if I don't get what I want."

"I-I can't," Jacobs said, his voice now trembling.

"Yes, you can!" Vogler shouted.

"What do you want from me?" Jacobs shouted back.

Vogler stood and turned his back to Jacobs and smiled to himself. How quickly they give in, he thought, although he was a little disappointed. He was hoping Jacobs would have had the character to resist a little longer.

"I want information," he calmly said as he sat back down at the desk. "Let's start with something simple. Tell me about one of your missions, the one right before you got shot down."

This is the moment of truth, Jacobs thought. If he talked to the German he would live, but could he live with himself if he did? Would it make him a traitor or just a survivor? The major already seemed to know everything there was to know about him, so why did he want to know about his second to last mission? Did he already know the answers and just want to test him or did he really not know?

He didn't want to die, but living with the reality that he had betrayed his friends and his country would not be a life worth living. He sat up a little straighter in his chair and gathered all the courage he could muster. "Jacobs, William H. Serial number..."

Vogler's face remained emotionless, but inwardly he was smiling. He was happy to see that Jacobs was stronger than he originally thought and happy to see that the interrogation would go to the next level.

"Very well then, have it your way. Guards!" Vogler shouted and immediately two SS guards came into the room and without speaking or even acknowledging Vogler, they grabbed Jacob's arms and tied them to the chair, bound his feet and then left as swiftly as they had entered.

Vogler leaned forward and opened the bottom desk drawer, took out a glass and set it on the desk, then reached back down and took out a decanter, poured some of the liquid into the glass and placed the decanter down next to the glass.

The SS Major raised the glass in a mock salute, then drank. "This is Höhler whiskey, though I doubt you have heard of it, being a German brand. I prefer it to your American whiskeys; it has a subtler, smoother taste to it, not like, what do you call it, moonshine?"

He set the glass down then opened another drawer and pulled out a rolled leather tool pouch. He set it on the desk, carefully untied the leather strings and meticulously unrolled it in front of Jacobs.

The eyes of the young flyer grew to twice their normal size when Vogler finished unwrapping the case. Laid out in front of him, set against the black velvet interior of the case, was a row of twelve highly polished stainless steel instruments. He wasn't familiar with some of their unusual shapes, but what he did recognize scared the hell out of him.

Vogler learned back in his chair, resting his chin in his hand and tapping his finger on his lips, contemplating which instrument he should choose first.

Jacobs watched in horror as he slipped the first item from the case. It was some sort of two-edged knife that had a long thin blade that curved upward at the tip. The open side of the blade was smooth while the back side was serrated for cutting. Vogler held the knife up, letting the light sparkle and shine off its polished surface, then placed it on the table in front of Jacobs, with the blade pointing at him.

Vogler did this with each of the instruments, carefully selecting them and placing them in specific order on the table. Some were thin and flat, others had serrated edges and others had a totally foreign look to them, but the last one that Vogler placed on the table made Jacobs' heart stop. It had a wide, flat blade that was crescent shaped. He recognized it from growing up on a farm and from hunting. It was a skinning blade.

Satisfied with the order in which he had laid out his instruments, Vogler poured another glass of whiskey and drank it. When he was finished, he set the glass down and simply got up and walked out of the room without saying a word or even looking at the frightened prisoner.

CHAPTER SEVENTEEN

"Oui," Franc said, looking at the three Americans standing in front of him, "I shouldn't be telling you this, but there is a large operation tonight and we are shorthanded and need everyone for the mission. We will hide you and try to smuggle you and your men out within the next day or two."

"Can we help?" Perry asked. "We can't ask you to risk your lives for us while we just sit and hide, and besides, we are still soldiers."

Franc paused and considered the request. "It will be dangerous."

"Like what we do now isn't dangerous?" Perry smiled.

"You have a point, Captain, but this is a different kind of danger."

Perry nodded. "True, but we are willing nonetheless."

"I will discuss your offer with the others. We will have some food brought in and you need to get some rest in either case. Please stay here in the barn."

Perry and the other nodded as Franc and Claude left, closing the barn door behind them.

At 11:30 that evening, the barn door opened and four men walked in, each carrying a submachine gun. Perry and his two companions stood and waited for their fate to be decided.

"We have discussed the matter," Franc said. "Are you and your companions sure you want to do this? We cannot guarantee your safety."

Perry nodded. "We understand and we still want to help."

The Frenchman smiled. "I am glad to hear that. Come."

They all gathered around a small work bench as Franc unrolled a set of plans.

"This is the Gestapo Headquarters here in town. It used to be the library but the Nazis took it over when they invaded our country. The Allies are very close now, and the Germans are in full, if not panicked, retreat. Along with destroying bridges and burning buildings to hinder the Allies' advance, the Gestapo is trying to cover their tracks by destroying all the evidence of their atrocities, including what they have done with people they have taken prisoner.

"We know they have at least five prisoners, maybe more, being held in the lower levels of the library right now. We need to get them out tonight before they are killed."

Perry nodded. "How many troops are guarding the building?"

"There are two here," Franc said, pointing at the diagram, "at the main entrance, plus no more than one or two inside at this time of night."

"Well that doesn't seem too bad," Gibbler added.

"Oui, but there is a small garrison of about thirty men bivouacking here in the hotel just around the corner. If the guards in the library manage to sound the alarm, we would soon be overwhelmed."

"What's your plan then?" Perry asked.

"Julien here," Franc nodded toward a grey haired man in his mid-sixties, "helped build the original building and has helped with several renovations over the years, and can get us in through one of the chutes they used to pour coal down when the building had a coal boiler for heat.

"We will post you and your men across the street from the hotel in case the alarm is sounded. That way you can ambush the soldiers as they come running out."

Perry studied the drawings for a moment, then spoke. "Why don't we go with you and Julien instead, and have your men cover the entrance? This is your town, if there is trouble and they have to retreat, they know the streets, where to hide and not to hide, and who they can trust."

Franc looked at his companions and they all nodded in agreement. "Very well then, it is settled."

"When do we leave?" Perry asked.

"Now."

Perry and Gibbler looked at each other with apprehension as they were each handed a submachine gun and two clips of ammunition. Mitchell, however, grabbed the gun with delight. He examined the weapon closely, looked along the sights, then pulled back the bolt, checking the action. A big smile lighted his face. "Can I keep this after we're done?"

"A boy and his toys." Perry said, shaking his head. "Get in the car."

The plan was discussed and each man's responsibilities laid out, but for the most part, the ride into town was relatively quiet.

They dropped Franc's two men three blocks from the hotel while they parked in a nearby alley at the back of the library, pulling in behind another parked car.

"This is a spare car," Franc said, "in case there are more prisoners we don't know about." Franc turned off the key, then looked at the three American airmen sitting in the back seat. "This is, how you say, the point of no return."

"I appreciate it," Perry said, "but we're still going in."

"Good, let's go then."

CHAPTER EIGHTEEN

It was early evening by the time Ramos and Idleman found a good place to hide on a little knoll overlooking what was left of the rail center on the outskirts of the city. With a small measure of satisfaction, they looked at the rail tracks, twisted like spaghetti, knowing that their bombs or bombs from a fellow squadron had turned this once important shipping center of the Third Reich into nothing more than a scrap yard.

There was only one line working and they'd seen the train come through just before dusk. There were several guards on top of each railcar and it had stopped only long enough to get another load of coal. As the train pulled to a stop, a multitude of hands and arms stuck out from the few small slots that ran along the top of the sides of each boxcar.

"What do you make of that?" Idleman asked.

"I don't know, a prisoner train maybe?"

"Whoever they are, they must be hot in there. There are no air vents in the roof and only those little air slots. And look at the way those guys are pushing and shoving against the slots."

The pair were close enough to hear muffled shouts escaping through the bars and neither man needed a degree in a foreign language to know that the cries that emanated from the boxcars were pleas for help.

The guards walked along the tracks yelling at the prisoners and hitting at their hands with their rifle butts, smashing them against the side of the railcar; another guard took a bucket of water and threw it into the window. The boxcar rocked back and forth as its inhabitants fought for those few precious drops.

This amused some of the guards and they took it a step further and began throwing chunks of bread through the windows, like they were feeding animals in a zoo. Even from their distant vantage point, the Americans could hear the panic as the human wave surged inside the car, trying to get the morsels of bread.

"Bastards!" Ramos said, looking at the Nazi guards. Idleman nodded his head in agreement. "Yeah, I hope those poor souls get to wherever they're going soon."

Ramos and Idleman watched helplessly as the guards tormented the prisoners for the next half-hour until they finally had enough coal and the train slowly pulled away.

Evening fell and much of the city remained dark for fear of attracting the wrath of the British bombers. A few traces of light could be seen poking out from poorly covered windows and there were a few small fires scattered about.

"Okay, what's the plan?" Idleman asked.

"We've got to get out of these uniforms and into some civilian clothes if we want to have a hope of surviving. First thing is to ditch our flight jackets. They identify us too easily as downed pilots. Next, we work our way into the old downtown section of the city."

"To find the resistance?"

"No, to find clothes."

Idleman look at his friend with a "are you nuts?" look.

Ramos just smiled. "Trust me on this one. Look at us, we're bruised and beaten up and generally a mess. We don't look like gentlemen nor could we pass ourselves off as gentlemen. We look like bums and so we'll dress like bums. And where do you find the most bums in any city? Downtown, that's where. We'll roll a couple of winos, take their clothes and blend in with the rest of the bums that no one ever pays any attention to. Once we do that, we keep our eyes and ears open and with a little luck, we'll find the resistance."

"Doesn't sound like much of a plan to me," Idleman said.

"Oh yeah, you got a better one?"

"No," Idleman had to admit.

"Good, then let's get going."

They took off their jackets and buried them under a nearby bush. "Come on," Ramos said. They slipped over the embankment, sliding down the hill, weaving their way between the bushes, using them for cover. Once down, they ran along the tracks and hid in the torn and twisted remains of railcars and locomotives that had been torn apart by the bombings.

By now it was very dark, making it dangerous to move through the wreckage. Jagged pieces of metal, charred black from fire, blended perfectly into the night, forming deadly fingers eager to tear open clothing or flesh.

The pair followed the tracks through the warehouse and industrial districts and into the older part of the city. The Americans hid behind a pile of rubble and watched and waited. A pair of civilians, a man and a woman, walked down the street, ignoring two men who were asleep in a doorway. Next, three German officers, obviously drunk, staggered down the sidewalk and they too ignored the men huddled in the doorway.

"See, what'd I tell ya?" Ramos whispered. "Bums are the people you see and yet you don't see. For whatever reason, they get ignored, which is perfect for us. We'll be hidden in plain sight and that's exactly why the resistance will be down here too, because they can move without being suspicious. Look, over there!" Ramos pointed over Idleman's shoulder. "Those two going down that alley. They look about our size. Come on, we'll knock 'em out and take their clothes."

The street was empty at that moment except for two other transients at the end of the block, warming themselves over a fire burning in a barrel. The Americans ran low across the street and hid alongside one of the empty stoops. They walked along the building and peered around the corner down the alleyway. Both of the drifters were staggering down the middle of the alley, leaning on each other for support. One stopped and tipped up a bottle he had hidden in a paper sack. His friend tried to grab it from him and they started to argue.

Seeing their chance, the two flyers rushed forward and took the two by surprise. Ramos dispatched his man with a solid right hook square to the jaw. Idleman swung wide at his man, hitting him on the side of the face, just in front of his ear. Idleman grabbed his hand, while the man grabbed the side of his face and let out a shout of pain.

Ramos quickly silenced the man with another knockout blow. "What's the matter with you?" Ramos whispered. "Haven't you ever been in a fight before?"

"Yes," Idleman replied, trying to sound tough. "No, not really," he truthfully admitted, shaking the pain out of his knuckles. Ramos just looked at him dumbfounded.

"Really? You've never been in a fight before? Not even with your brothers?" He found that very hard to believe since fighting was a way of life for him. He thought everyone knew how to fight.

"Sure, I fought with my brothers, wrestled with them and stuff, but we never hit each other. Pa would have really cleaned our clocks if did that."

Ramos just shook his head. "Okay, help me drag them over into the corner and we'll take their clothes."

"Man, these guys stink," Idleman said.

"All the better for us. Who's going to want to get close to someone who stinks just to check their papers?"

"True, but still..."

"Oh shut up, and hurry up and change."

They stripped the two men of their shirts and pants and quickly got out of their own clothes and put on the transients'. Ramos was a perfect fit, while Idleman's shirt was tight across the chest and the sleeves were too short. His pants were also too short by a couple of inches, giving him the look of a poorly dressed school child. Ramos looked at him and couldn't help but laugh.

"Very funny," Idleman snickered back.

"Sorry, man," Ramos replied, trying to stifle another laugh. He took the bottle out of the bag and smelled it, then quickly pulled it away from his nose. "Man, this stuff is bad." He took a swig and coughed hard, then took another. "Oh that burns. Want some?"

Without hesitation, Idleman grabbed the bottle and tipped it up, taking a huge gulp. He took the bottle from his lips and ended it with a satisfying "AAAAAAHHHHHHHH."

"Not bad," he said, handing the bottle back to his bewildered friend. "I may not know how to fight, but I do know how to drink."

Ramos just smiled and shook his head as he took the bottle back. He poured a little into his hand then splashed it on his face and neck like after-shave.

"Hey, what gives?" Idleman protested. "It wasn't that bad."

"All part of the plan, my friend. The worse we smell, the greater the chance they'll leave us alone."

Idleman nodded his head in agreement, took another drink and applied the rest of the alcohol to his face as if he were getting ready to go out on a date. "Now what?" he asked.

"We ditch our clothes a few blocks from here, then find a place to sleep." Idleman followed Ramos down the alley and around the corner. They walked two blocks and turned into another alley where they dumped their clothes then walked out the other end.

As they turned the corner, Ramos bounced off something, then hit the ground. It was if the side of the building had stepped out in front of him. But as he fell, he saw that the building that hit him wore boots. Ramos quickly extinguished the fire of anger in his eyes when he saw that the boots of the walking building belonged to a German soldier.

For a moment, the two surprised men just stared at each other, then Ramos got to his feet and smiled, then threw himself at the soldier like he was hugging a long lost friend. The German at first didn't know what to do, but as soon as he caught of whiff of the 100 proof perfume, he swore and pushed the man aside. Ramos fell to the ground laughing, pretending to be drunk.

Idleman came around the corner just as his friend hit the ground and froze in terror when he saw not only the fat soldier in front of him, but that several others were also coming their way. In terror he looked down at his friend thinking he had lost his mind, then he saw Ramos wink at him and he understood.

Idleman started laughing too and pointed at his friend on the ground, then reached out to hug the fat German but stopped short when he brought up his rifle and pointed it at him. Both men stopped laughing, then Idleman let out a great roar as if he had just heard the funniest joke in the world. He pointed at the rifle, then pretended to shoot his own make-believe gun. He "shot" the soldier in front of him, then shot the rest of the squad. He pointed down and "shot" his friend, then shot down imaginary planes, all while laughing and staggering around.

The big soldier loosened his grip on the rifle, and turned to his friends and laughed. He twirled his finger around his head and looked back at the laughing drunks. "Dumkopfs," he said, shaking his head. He shoved Idleman out of the way, then walked on past. Idleman hit the building wall and collapsed to the ground next to his friend. He sat slouched against the wall, pretending to be dazed as the soldiers walked past. He shot a quick glance at Ramos, who was still giggling.

The large soldier disappeared around the corner into the alley followed by his three comrades, all ignoring the two drunks. The fourth soldier, a lieutenant, stopped in front of Ramos. Ramos looked up to see a pair of dark eyes filled with hate staring down at him. He quickly looked away, not wanting to reveal the fear in his own eyes. The lieutenant kicked him in the foot and shouted some command that he didn't understand. When he didn't move, the lieutenant kicked him again, only much harder. Ramos let out a yelp of pain.

On the third kick, Ramos struggled to get up, but pretended he was too drunk to stand, hoping the officer would leave him alone.

Idleman watched as the German officer shouted at Ramos. He wasn't sure if the German suspected them or was just taking his anger out on the easiest target. Idleman knew he had to do something. He staggered to his feet and smiled as he took a step toward the officer with his arms open wide.

The German smiled back, which caught Idleman completely off guard. Idleman took another step forward when the soldier swung a quick right fist that hit him squarely on the jaw. The blow sent the American crashing against the wall and he crumpled back to the ground next to Ramos.

Ramos wanted to spring to his feet and beat this arrogant German to a bloody pulp, but he knew that if he fought back they were both as good as dead.

The German stood over them, fists clenched, ready and waiting for a fight, but none came. Clearly disappointed, he spit on the ground in front of them. He had just turned to leave when something caught his eye. The German lieutenant looked at the boots the drunks were wearing. They were well made and in good shape, and they didn't match the rest of their ragged and torn clothes. These were not the shoes of common drunks. Rage, anger and a strange sense of joy boiled in his soul. It spilled over in the form of a tiny, sinister smile. These were the escaped Americans, and they were his.

CHAPTER NINETEEN

Suddenly, silver ribbons of light pierced the night skies and the silence of the still air was shattered by the wail of air raid sirens. In that instant of distraction, Ramos swung his leg around, kicking the legs out from under the German. With a speed borne of desperation, Ramos jumped on top of the German and began hitting him with a flurry of lefts and rights.

The officer was taken by surprise and managed to block a few of the swings, but was no match for the street kid from LA. "Come on!" Idleman shouted as he grabbed Ramos by the arm. "We've got to get out of here!" Ramos stopped hitting the German and stood up, towering over his bleeding antagonist. He left the German with a parting gift as he gave him one last kick to the ribs before they ran.

The fleeing Americans had just turned the corner going down another alleyway when they heard shouting behind them, and gunfire. A bullet went high and wide, ricocheting off the wall two feet above their heads. The pair ducked and raced through the deserted streets and dashed into an open doorway.

From the street, the building looked intact, but once through the doorway, they could see that the building had taken a direct bomb hit. The roof was gone and the back wall had collapsed, leaving a unique view of the sky. They scrambled up and over and around the rubble and debris, and made their way up to the second floor and hid in what had once been a bedroom.

The bed was crushed by a huge timber beam that had fallen across it, and the dresser was a pile of kindling, smashed by a large chunk of stone that had once been part of the outside wall. Amidst the destruction and carnage, there stood an oddity that defied the very meaning of war.

A vanity sat in the corner by the door, one leg broken and the top smashed and covered with chunks of plaster and wood splinters. But the mirror stood proud and erect, not a scratch on it. In fact, the dust had not touched it and the beams from the searchlights bounced off it, immersing the room in a dull and eerie light.

The two escapees crouched in the corner and watched the show unfolding before them, forgetting the immediate danger. They could hear the distant drone of the aircraft overhead. They guessed there were about 100 British Lancasters and that they were coming in fairly low at around 10,000 feet. Sporadic anti-aircraft fire now thundered from the ring of guns set up around the city.

Idleman sat and listened as they fired: so that's what they sound like, he thought. He had witnessed firsthand their deadly results from the sky, but had never thought about what they sounded like when they went off. They were louder than he could have imagined.

The silver beams of the searchlights crisscrossed the sky, looking for the invading bombers. One of the lights found one of the British planes as its made it way in the dark. Soon, three more lights locked on, dragging the luckless plane out of the safety of darkness and exposing it to the crosshairs of the gunners.

With a visible enemy to take out their fury on, the guns began pounding out their drumbeat of death in unison. Black puffs of smoke reached out to surround the plane as the shells exploded, getting closer and closer with each volley. One of the shells scored a direct hit on the left wing. The fuel cells exploded, and for an instant, the glow of the explosion dimmed the brightness of the searchlights, then vanished. With nothing but a dark hole left in the sky, the lights began weaving across the sky again, searching for another plane to entangle in their snare.

Deafening was too weak a word to use when the first bomb exploded. When he was a kid, Idleman loved reading about the Old West and the stories about the Indians hunting buffalos on the Great Plains. He would read how there were once herds that numbered into the thousands and the ground shook under their hooves and that the sound was thunderous. The rumble he heard charging toward them now would have struck fear into even the bravest Indian warrior's heart.

The rail yard where they had been earlier in the day was in the vicinity where the first bombs hit. The bombs were "walking" their way toward the center of the city, towards them.

One of the searchlights dropped low for a moment and its beam sliced through the building they were in. For a brief moment, Idleman could see a painting on the wall. It was a picture of a frightened man whose eyes were full of fear and uncertainty. Then, in an instant, he realized that it wasn't a picture, but a reflection, his reflection, in the vanity mirror. It was hard to believe that the distraught face starring back at him was his own. Did he really look like that?

He could see the explosions of the bombs as they drew closer. Brilliant flashes of light drove back the darkness as they detonated, each coming closer and closer, flashing like dozens of sunrises. But instead of bringing a new day, they were bringing death.

The explosions were erratic, not rhythmic, adding to the terror. Some of the planes had dropped all their bombs at once, creating a string of explosions, while others dropped in salvoes, two or three at a time, extending the range of destruction and terror. The random detonations only added to the uncertainty of being hit or missed, living or dying.

The bombs were falling into the heart of the city now, shaking the ground like a giant rolling earthquake. BOOM... BOOM... BOOM... BOOM... BOOM was the steady pounding of Hell's Anvil as sparks flew, lighting up the city with each strike. The very Earth itself trembled under each terrible blow.

But far more frightening than the sight was the sound. The noise was truly unbelievable and it hurt his ears each time a bomb exploded. Every blast produced its own concussion wave that could not only be felt in the swaying of the building but in the pit of the stomach.

The roar was more than just deafening, it was maddening, blocking out all other noise. Even the very thoughts in his head were pounded into incoherent mush. Yes, he could believe that the frightened face in the mirror was his. He felt like screaming, but then, no one could hear him, not even himself.

For him, the war, his war, was fought at 20,000 feet, plane against plane, not man against man. If they shot down an attacking fighter, they destroyed an aircraft, not a human being. If their target was a ball bearing plant, then their mission was to destroy the factory; he had never really thought that much about the people inside. He had never given much thought to what his plane crew did or what effects their bombs had, other than knocking out the target.

But going from 20,000 feet to ground zero had a way of changing one's perspective. He could see a string of bombs exploding down the street, each detonation drawing closer and closer, exploding with the steady rhythm of a drum beat. He could tell by the pattern that the house they were in was right in the path of the falling bombs.

Idleman could feel the wall he was leaning against vibrate and pulse with each approaching blast. Bits of debris and dust fell, shaken loose by the shivering house. The house and his world were falling apart. He glanced again at the mirror, his image trembling as the vanity danced across the shaking floor. His jittery reflection mirrored the way he felt. Damn the British for their nighttime saturation bombing.

He looked over at Ramos. He was sitting on the floor with his knees pulled up to his chest, covering his ears with both hands, eyes shut tight. He didn't appear to be overly concerned or scared, just annoyed by the dust and noise. Sometimes he really admired Ramos for his seemingly unwavering nerve.

Ramos was angry and frustrated. He hated being helpless, watching everything going on around him and not being able to do anything about it. Not being able to control his own future. He should be the one up there dropping the bombs, not running around on the ground and hiding in an old bombed out building.

And the light, the brilliant, blinding flashes of light that appeared when the bombs exploded, was made worse by the dark. He could handle the noise. He'd grown up in the city, so sudden or loud noises didn't really bother him much, even if this noise was VERY loud. In fact, he preferred noise to the quiet, but the flashing lights really bothered him. Every time someone took a picture with a flashbulb, he wanted to go through the ceiling. He didn't know why it bothered him so much, probably some childhood thing, but it really didn't matter. Closing his eyes didn't help much either because he could see the flashes through his eyelids.

He stole a quick look at his friend sitting beside him. Idleman seemed unruffled, taking everything in stride. Sometimes he admired that country boy for his patience and calm.

A 500-pound general-purpose bomb plunged into the house two doors down the street. The force of the explosion slapped the wall they were leaning against, sending them sprawling onto the floor in the middle of the room. The mortar that held the stone building together shattered and exploded into the room like a shotgun blast.

One of the mortar projectiles shattered the vanity mirror that had survived so many earlier bombings. Large shards of glass were scattered on the floor. Because the roof was open, the fragments reflected the crossing searchlights and exploding shells, making it look like silent fireworks were going off in the room.

The runaways could hear the sound of destruction trailing off in the distance as the bomber formation moved on. The pair starred at each other in a daze until Ramos finally spoke.

"Are you okay, man?"

"Yeah, I think so," Idleman replied, shaking his head. "I like being up there better than being down here." He smiled weakly.

Ramos nodded. "I'm with you on that one."

"Are your ears ringing?"

"Like church bells on Sunday morning."

"Church bells? Since when did you ever go to church?"

"Hey, I went to church every Sunday until I got caught smoking in the confessional."

Idleman just looked at his friend, smiling and shaking his head.

Just then they heard a noise and whispered talking coming from downstairs.

"Come on, we've got to get out of here," Ramos whispered and tilted his head toward the window. The whispers quickly turned to shouting and two gunshots rang out.

Both men hurled themselves out the window and landed with a thud on the roof of the next house. Just as they landed, the roof, weakened by the bombing, gave way and collapsed underneath them.

The entire section of the roof that Ramos was standing on gave way and he was able to slide down the giant slab onto the floor unhurt. Idleman, however, was not so lucky. The support beam under where he was standing snapped, literally dropping that entire section of the roof straight down.

Idleman landed hard among the falling timbers and plaster. He shattered his left ankle as he landed, and the injury was compounded by a crossbeam that fell on his leg, pinning him to the floor. Idleman howled in pain as the beam smashed his leg. Even before the dust settled, Ramos had rushed over to help his friend.

"Hang on, man!" Ramos said. "I'll get you out of here."

Idleman coughed and shook his head. "Forget it, I'm not going anywhere. You need to get yourself out of here. The Krauts will be here any minute." As if to punctuate his point, they heard more shouting.

"Shut up!" Ramos snapped, then reached down and grabbed the beam. Idleman tried but couldn't stifle a cry of pain as his friend starting lifting.

"Go, just go! You can get away."

"I'm not leaving without you."

"I'll just slow you down."

"Just shut up and pull your leg out when I tell you to." Straining with everything he had, Ramos managed to lift the beam and Idleman was just able to get his leg free before Ramos' grip slipped and it smashed back on the floor.

"Come on!" Ramos hoisted his friend's arm over his shoulder and started dragging him out. They managed to pick their way through the rubble and debris and reach the doorway at the far end of the building, all the while being chased by the sound of shouting soldiers closing in on them. Idleman was cringing in pain as they reached the doorway.

"You've got to go on without me, Tony. I can barely move."

"I already told you I'm not leaving you behind," Ramos said as he peered around the corner.

Idleman grabbed his friend by the arm and yanked him back inside. "Listen to me, you thick-headed idiot! I can't run, but you can."

"I can't leave you here to be captured."

"And I can't let you get caught because of me."

"Are you deaf or just stupid? I said I'm not leaving you."

Idleman sighed. "Okay, okay, you win. Look, see that building across the street?" Ramos nodded. "Good, I think if we can get to there, we can snake our way through the ruins to the rail yard, then back into the woods."

Ramos nodded again. "Yeah, I think you're right."

"Good, now run over and find a place for us to hide, then come back and get me. But before you go, hand me that board over there so I can use it as a crutch."

Ramos grabbed the board and handed it to his friend. "Here ya go. Just sit tight and stay quiet, and I'll be right back."

Idleman gave him gave him a thumbs up. "Okay, now get going!"

Ramos nodded, checked to see that the coast was clear, then sprinted across the street. Idleman watched as his friend took off, but Ramos was only halfway across the street when he saw a German solider coming around the corner of the building. It was the same huge man they had literally run into earlier that evening.

Idleman let out a huge sigh of relief as the big German didn't see Ramos. As soon as he rounded the corner, he stopped and lit a cigarette. Ramos was safe but he knew there was now no way he could get across the street, and he also knew that his stubborn friend would not leave without him.

Idleman stood on his makeshift crutch and took a deep breath; he didn't want to do this but he knew it was the only way that Ramos would stand a chance. He stepped out onto the street and started shouting.

"Hey, over here!" he shouted as he hobbled away from the German as fast as he could. "You big, fat, ugly slob, you can't catch me." He looked back and saw the startled expression on the German's face and couldn't help but smile. He continued shouting as he limped down the street. "Run, Ramos, you idiot, run! This is your chance to get away, now run!"

Ramos had just ducked into the shadows and was shocked to see a German soldier suddenly appear from around the corner. He watched in relief as the soldier didn't raise any alarms as he casually stood there and lit up a smoke. But his relief turned to dismay then horror as he saw his friend step out of hiding and start shouting.

"You crazy son of a..." Ramos muttered under his breath, shaking his head. "You always had to have the last word." For a fleeting second, the eyes of the two airmen met and a world of understanding passed between. Then Ramos disappeared into the shadows and a small smile crossed Idleman's lips.

CHAPTER TWENTY

Idleman was moving fast for a three-legged man, and for a brief moment he thought he just might be able to outrun the fat German. But those thoughts were crushed as three soldiers came rushing around the corner toward him. Knowing there was no place to run or hide, he dropped his crutch and raised his hands in surrender.

He was quickly surrounded and they all stood in silence as Lieutenant Shubert and Sergeant Bauer emerged through the side of the building where Idleman and Ramos had been hiding.

The lieutenant walked over with long, powerful strides, and without saying a word, viciously kicked Idleman's feet out from under him. The American landed hard on his injured leg and a sharp cry of pain escaped from his lips.

"I'm an American flyer," Idleman said between clenched teeth, fighting back the pain. "I was shot down two days ago."

"You killed one of my men earlier today," the lieutenant spit out, then kicked him again even harder.

"I'm sorry," Idleman said quietly, remorse filling his voice.

This seemed to make the German officer even angrier as he started kicking Idleman over and over. The squad of soldiers looked at each other, as Shubert viciously attacked the man lying on the ground. They knew it wasn't right for him to be beating the prisoner, but they were afraid to say anything.

"Sir?" one of the men said sheepishly. "Shouldn't we take the prisoner to the Stalag?" When the lieutenant didn't answer, he repeated himself and gently put his hand on the man's shoulder.

The lieutenant swung around, immediately drew his pistol and pointed it at the soldier. "Do not tell me what to do!" he shouted. "This man killed a proud and brave solider, and he will pay the price for it!"

A car drove by, slowing down to take a look, then continued on. A moment later, a staff car rounded the corner and stopped. An SS major stepped out of the car and calmly walked over. Everyone snapped to attention except the lieutenant, who was still seething with rage.

"What is going on here, Lieutenant?" the major asked, emphasizing that he outranked him. The lieutenant controlled his rage and snapped to attention.

"We are interrogating a spy, sir!"

Major Vogler smiled. "I know interrogations, Lieutenant, and this is not an interrogation; it's a beating." Vogler stepped over and looked at the man lying on the ground. "Are you a spy?" he asked.

Idleman looked up and the major and shook his head. "No, sir," he said weakly. "I'm a downed American flyer."

"And did you tell the lieutenant that?"

"Yes, sir."

"Well?" Vogler said, looking at the officer.

"Earlier today we tracked him and two of his companions. We chased and killed one." He paused for a moment, then quickly added, "Who resisted capture, only to return and find that he had killed one of my soldiers." Shubert looked down with disgust at the prisoner.

Idleman felt a sharp pain, only it wasn't from the German's boot, but hearing of the loss of his friend, that Joe Thomas had been killed. He had heard the gunshot but had hoped that it had been something else. Now he knew it wasn't.

Vogler turned from the lieutenant and looked at the large German standing behind the other. "You there, Private, was the man who was shot wearing an American uniform?"

Suddenly Otto Faust found himself in the spotlight again, only this time he didn't want it. He couldn't lie to the major, nor could he tell the truth because he knew that the lieutenant would punish him for it later. Both men looked expectantly at him, and he could feel the sweat forming on his forehead: what should he do? Instead the lieutenant spoke, and Faust felt like he was going to pass out from relief.

"This man here is not wearing a uniform and any soldier caught behind enemy lines without his uniform is to be considered a spy and shot."

"So you think he really is a spy then?"

"Yes, sir, that is why I was interrogating him."

"If he is a spy as you say, are you qualified to be the one interrogating him? Do you know the right questions to ask? Do you know who to give that information to once you have extracted it?" Vogler looked at the American lying on the ground then back at his tormentor. "This man is clearly not a spy and is plainly who he says he is. However, that does not mean that he may not have valuable information that we can use. But beating him?" Vogler shook his head. "Brute force and beatings rarely yield the desired effect. You see, I have some knowledge and expertise in these matters." A small sadistic smile crossed his lips.

"I cannot condone such actions. Brutality without purpose is so barbaric that it is an affront to my personal standards. The extraction and acquiring of information is a process to be enjoyed, the moment savored, not to be carried out in the middle of the street by swinging fists and kicking legs. It is to be conducted on a canvas that is fresh and new, one that is susceptible to the instruments of the interrogation, not one that is already battered, bruised and stained." Vogler sighed as he looked at Idleman, his mood turning melancholy.

"I could have learned so much from you," he said as he reached down and gently lifted Idleman's head, cradling his chin in his hand. "But your senseless beating by this cretin has ruined much of what I could have learned. Ironic as it seems, this amateur's beating," he looked at the lieutenant, "has probably saved your life."

Idleman was still lying on the ground in sheer agony, pain radiating through his broken body. At the moment, he didn't feel very lucky but by the way the major was talking, when he looked into the major's eyes, a shiver ran down his spine. He wasn't sure which fate was the lesser of two evils.

Vogler's mood suddenly changed as he turned. "I have a fresh canvas back at headquarters that needs my attention. Lieutenant, you will not harm this man any further, understood?"

"Yes, sir." A less than enthusiastic reply.

Vogler frowned, then continued. "Furthermore, you will take him directly to Stalag 11 and personally deliver him to Colonel Tommler who is a friend of mine. There will be no 'accidents' along the way. Do I make myself clear, Lieutenant?"

"Yes sir!"

"Good," Vogler said with a slight smile, then looked down at the American. "Enjoy your stay at Stalag 11, Sergeant. You'll find Colonel Tommler to be a tough but fair man." Vogler got back in the car, then rolled down his window. "I'll want your name so that when I call Colonel Tommler I can confirm your arrival."

"Idleman, sir. Sergeant Jerry Idleman."

"Very well." Vogler started to roll up his window but stopped and looked at the American, a smile of recognition coming to this face.

"A change of plans," Vogler said, looking at Shubert. "I will take the prisoner with me. Put him in the back seat."

"Sir?"

"Are you deaf or just an imbecile? I said I am taking him with me. You there, Private," Vogler said, looking at Faust, "the one who likes to eat too much strudel, pick up the prisoner and put him in the car."

Faust hesitated as he nervously glanced at Lieutenant Shubert.

"NOW!"

Faust jumped. "Yes, sir!" He quickly reached down and helped the American to his feet, then bundled him into the car.

As they drove off, Vogler turned around and looked at his prisoner. "Well, Mr. Idleman, I have someone who will be dying to see you."

CHAPTER TWENTY-ONE

Ramos had to admit that Jerry was right, but that still didn't make it any easier to leave him to the Germans. With one last look at his friend hobbling down the street, he turned and made his way deeper into the building.

He hurried as fast as he could through the bombed out building, filled with a new sense of urgency to escape, vowing that he would not let his friend's sacrifice be in vain.

The back half of the building was in shambles, only one corner section still standing. He weaved in and out of the rubble, making his way to the corner. Crouched in the shadows, he peered out and saw the street empty. In the distance, he could hear the shouts of the soldiers echoing through the alleyways and bouncing off the remains of the buildings.

He was halfway across the street, heading to the next building, when a black car suddenly appeared out of nowhere and screeched to a halt in front of him. He froze in terror, waiting for the car door to fly open and storm troopers to rush out and take him prisoner. The door did fly open, but there were no German soldiers.

"American, yes?" the driver shouted. Ramos just stood there, not knowing what to say. Again, the driver called out. "You, American, quick, get in, get in. Resistance!" He pointed to himself. "I'm with the resistance, now hurry, hurry, get in."

"Halt! Halt!"

Ramos turned to see three German soldiers rounding the corner of the building, shouting and running toward him. Needing no more encouragement, he jumped into the car. He was thrown back in the seat as the driver squealed the tires. Ramos turned and looked back at the soldiers as he sped away.

"Lucky for you I came along," the driver said as they whipped around a corner and disappeared into the night.

"Thank you," Ramos said, looking at the driver, "but how did you know I was an American?"

"I was driving by when I heard your friend shouting in English, so I knew you had to be Americans. A downed flyer?"

Ramos nodded.

"I thought so." The car slowed and they made several turns.

"Can you help me escape? My name is Tony, by the way."

"Oui." The driver nodded. "I will take you to some friends of mine. My name is Jacques."

"How long until I can get out of here?"

The Frenchman shrugged his shoulders. "It will be difficult, but we should be able to take care of you tonight."

"Tonight? Really? That would be great. How much farther?"

"Relax, we'll soon be there." Jacques smiled.

Ramos nodded and sat quietly as they drove on, making several more turns.

"Quick, pull the car over!" Ramos suddenly shouted. "I think I'm going to be sick."

"Please, monsieur, we are almost there."

Ramos quickly covered his mouth with his hands. "Pull over, now!"

With a snarl, Jacques pulled the car over to the side of the road. He put it in neutral and turned to his passenger.

"Hurry up," was all he managed to get out before a strong right fist from Ramos snapped his head back.

"Who are you?" Ramos shouted as he grabbed the man. "You're not with the Resistance!"

"Please, monsieur, I don't know what you are talking about."

"Like hell you don't." Ramos hit him again then grabbed him by the back of the neck and slammed Jacques's head against the steering wheel. "You think I'm stupid? I'm a city boy, born and raised, and I know when I'm being taken for a ride. And how come there are no door lock pulls to lock and unlock the doors without a key? What are you trying to pull here?"

"Please, I was only trying to help..." the Frenchman pleaded, then suddenly reached down beside his seat with his left hand and pulled out a gun. Ramos started for it but Jacques swung his right elbow, hitting Ramos in the face, sending him sprawling across his seat. Jacques brought the gun around but the barrel hit the steering wheel, giving Ramos time to lift his foot and kick his opponent, slamming him hard against the door.

Ramos bounced back and grabbed the gun with one hand and threw a flurry of jabs with the other. Jacques blocked a few and succeeded in getting in a few blows of his own. The Frenchman managed to get up on the seat and use his weight advantage to push his smaller opponent down onto the seat.

Ramos was struggling now. He still had one hand on the gun but the other was no longer throwing punches, but was straining to push the big man back. Ramos could smell the Frenchman's foul breath, matched only by his smug leer as the barrel of the gun slowly began moving toward his chest.

There was a muffled explosion... and the struggle stopped.

CHAPTER TWENTY-TWO

Ramos took one gasp of air, then summoned all his strength and shoved the dead body of the French traitor off him. At the last possible moment, he'd been able to twist his body and use his opponent's leverage against him and point the barrel of the gun up as it fired.

Ramos sat in the front seat, shaking. He had been in many fights, but despite his tough guy image, he had never killed anyone before. Slowly his nerves began to settle and the reality of the situation started coming into focus. He was sitting in a car in the middle of a German city with a dead Frenchman lying beside him while half the German army looked for him, and his friend had sacrificed himself so he could escape. He sighed; two nights ago the only problem he had was whether to dance with the blonde or the brunette at the USO.

Ramos snapped himself out of his melancholy. He was a survivor and that's what he intended to do. Escape was the first order of business. The Germans were looking for an American on foot, so they wouldn't think to look at a passing car. The Frenchman also said they were close to the front lines, so he would drive west as far as he could, then ditch the car and walk the rest of the way.

Ramos took the gun and looked in the dead man's wallet and surprised to find several thousand francs in it. Betraying innocent men must be good business, Ramos thought as he shoved the money into his pocket. He didn't like the idea of taking blood money, but it might come in handy down the road.

Ramos heard the body hit the ground with a satisfying thud when he kicked it out of the car. With a nearly a full tank of fuel, he turned the car around and headed west, to freedom.

Ramos was grateful that it was night and the streets were empty because he got lost several times as he weaved his way through the unfamiliar city. Finally he reached the outskirts of town and headed out on what he hoped was the main east-west highway.

Though he loved the city, he was happy to be out in the country now. He smiled about the irony of his statement and thought of Jerry, and prayed that he'd be all right. He'd only been driving a few minutes when he saw multiple headlights up ahead. Was it a roadblock? Should he speed up and ram his way through, or ditch the car and try to make it on foot?

He could see that the headlights were moving so he decided to take a chance and stay with the car. Drawing closer, he could now see that it was a convoy moving in the opposite direction. He slowed and passed several staff cars followed by ten 6x6 troop trucks, all overloaded with troops, many of whom looked to be injured.

Fortunately, they didn't try to stop him; they barely seemed to notice him. Ramos smiled to himself: why should they care about one crazy car heading toward the advancing American lines instead of running away from them? With a sigh of relief, he passed the last truck in the convoy and once again owned the road.

Over the next hour, he passed several more convoys and knew he must be getting closer to the front lines because each of the convoys he passed was a little less organized than the one before; the last one being about twenty soldiers, all on foot, all with dirty and tattered uniforms, walking at a steady, hurried pace.

He drove for another ten minutes and decided he had pushed his luck as far as he could. He pulled over and stopped, got out of the car and started walking down the road. Soon, his feet were numb from walking. He trudged along, now walking on autopilot, disappointed that he hadn't come to the front lines yet. Had he taken a wrong turn somewhere? Maybe the Germans he had passed weren't running from the fight but going to it.

"Halt!"

Ramos froze in fear as the voice boomed in the night. How could he have been so careless, so stupid? It had never occurred to him that the Germans would keep a check point on the road.

He saw two shadowy figures rise out of the bushes and walk cautiously toward him, rifles at the ready. One stood on each side of him, sizing him up.

"Out for a little midnight stroll, Herr Hitler?" one of the guards said, laughing.

Ramos felt his knees go weak—they were speaking in English, they were Americans!

"Am I ever glad to see you guys!" Ramos said as he took a step forward and extended his hand.

Both soldiers took a step back, fingers twitching on the triggers. "Hold on there," one of the soldiers said. "Just because you speak English doesn't mean you're an American."

"What, you think I'm a Kraut? I'm an airman. I was the left waist gunner on a B-17, the *Red Light Lady*: we got shot down two days ago."

"Okay, smart guy, let's just see. Who won the World Series last year?"

"It was the Cards, but it should've been the Angels," Ramos replied.

"The Angels?" one said, looking suspiciously at Ramos. "There ain't no Angels in the National League."

"That's right, but they're still my team. I'm from L.A. and the Angels are in the Pacific Coast League."

"A farm club?" one of the soldiers said, almost laughing.

"Hey," Ramos said, clearly not happy that anyone would make fun of his team. "They scored 762 runs and won 100 games."

"Big deal," the soldier shot back, "the Cardinals scored 772 runs and had 105 wins!"

"Okay, okay," the other solider said, putting up his hands up. "I don't want you two to get in a fight over baseball. If this guy knows that much about a farm club then he has to be an American. Welcome home, buddy." All three men shook hands. "And besides, everyone knows that the Tigers should have won." He smiled.

"The Tigers, are you kidding me?

All three men started walking toward the American camp, arguing about baseball.

CHAPTER TWENTY-THREE

"Ah, Billy, so sorry to have kept you waiting." Vogler said as he walked back into the room as if he had been away for only a minute. Vogler was pleased at the expression that his American guest had etched upon his face. It was a combination of sheer terror, overwhelming anxiety, apprehension and doubt. Doubt not only if he could handle the torture and not break, but also doubt whether he would even make it out alive.

Though he wore his poker face, revealing nothing, Vogler was smiling on the inside. He had learned through trial and error and through many sessions that it wasn't the physical torture that usually got the results, it was the fear and anticipation of the torture that was the key.

He almost let slip a smile as he looked at the flyer sitting across from him. He wondered if the American realized that his hands were clenched in a white knuckled death grip on the arms of his chair.

"Now then, where were we? Ah, yes, you were going to tell me about your previous mission," Vogler said as he folded his hands on the desk in front of him.

Jacobs swallowed hard and tried to speak through his parched lips. His voice was steady but weak. "Jacobs, William H. Serial number... serial number..." Jacobs paused and realized to his shame and embarrassment that he had forgotten his serial number.

Jacobs swore under his breath then closed his eye and concentrated. "Jacobs, William H. Serial number 6335148."

"You still won't cooperate?" Vogler shook his head. "Guards!"

Jacobs braced himself, knowing that the last time they showed up they had tied him to the chair and he was afraid of what they might do this time. But instead of beating him, they dragged in another man who had a hood over his head and tied him in another chair.

Jacobs looked over at the man. It was easy to tell that he had been severely beaten from the blood staining his clothes. He sat slumped in the chair with his head hanging forward, his chin resting on his chest. Jacobs shuddered: is that what he had to look forward to?

Vogler stood and reached down, taking one of the instruments from the table. It had a long, thin blade looking like a letter opener or an ice pick. Vogler played with it as he spoke, coming around in front of the desk and sitting on its corner.

"Billy, we really don't have to go through all of this," he said as he held it up, letting the light reflect off the polished surface. "Now then, let's try this again, shall we? What was the target on your previous mission?"

"Jacobs, William H. Serial..." Before he could finish, he froze in terror as he saw Vogler stand, then raise his hand holding the knife and plunge it down. A shriek of pain filled the room as the knife went deep into the man's right leg.

Jacobs was stunned and felt nauseated as he looked at the knife protruding out from the thigh of the hooded man like a flag pole. Vogler released his grip, leaving the knife in the leg, and sat back down on the edge of the desk.

"I imagine from the cry that that was quite painful. I wonder if it will hurt just as much when I pull it out. Shall we see?"

Jacobs frantically shook his head but Vogler ignored him and reached over and pulled out the knife. Vogler looked disappointed when there was only a small yelp as he removed it.

"Well, I guess we now have the answer to that question," Vogler said as he took a cloth and wiped off the knife and carefully placed it back with the others.

"Do you feel like answering the question now or should I stab this man in his other leg?"

Jacobs drew in a deep breath. "I'm sorry, mister," he said, looking at the hooded man, "but I just can't answer his questions."

"I have found that a person can often endure suffering far beyond his expectations, but can't stand to let others suffer on his account, even if it is a stranger. But you are different, Billy, you're a real tough guy, huh? Letting this man take your punishment in the name of duty and honor."

"Please, I don't know anything."

"Now that's not the point here, is it?" Vogler asked as he picked up the skinning knife and walked over and stood behind the man. "You see all those instruments before you? Do you think I know how to use them?"

Jacobs nodded.

"Good, because I assure you that I am an expert with every one of them. You've proven your resolve not to talk even when a stranger is being tortured, but is your resolve still as strong if you know the person?"

Vogler ripped the hood off the bleeding man in the chair.

"Jerry!" Jacobs shouted, seeing his friend tied to the chair. "I'm sorry, Jerry. I didn't know, I didn't know it was you."

With great effort, Idleman slowly lifted his head and struggled out a half smile. “It’s okay, Billy,” he said weakly. “Don’t tell the bastard a thing.”

“Brave words,” Vogler said, “but can you live up to them?” He grabbed Idleman by the hair and pulled his head back and took the skinning knife and drew a thin line of blood as he moved it around Idleman’s scalp.

“Isn’t this what your American Indians used to do in the Old West? What do you think, Cowboy? Shall I keep going?”

Idleman tried to stifle a cry, but the pain was too great as the blade cut into his skin.

“Stop! I’ll tell you anything you want to know!” Jacobs shouted. “Just stop!”

“That wasn’t so hard, now was it?” Vogler said. “But I think you need to be taught a lesson in cooperation.” Vogler pulled Idleman’s head back again and brought the knife back up.

“Wait!” Jacobs pleaded. “I told you I would tell you whatever you wanted to know.”

“Yes, I know,” Vogler said very matter-of-factly, then continued to bring the knife up to Idleman's forehead. Just as he was about to cut and peel back the scalp, there was a muffled thud just outside the door.

Irritated at the interruption, Vogler reluctantly put the knife down and went to open the door. Just as he was reaching for the handle, he heard whispered voices floating down the corridor. He listened for a moment and realized that the Maquis were taking the building. He also realized that if they captured him, he was as good as dead. He had to act fast.

He quickly took out his pistol and clubbed each man over the head. He would use the knife later, killing them while they were unconscious and unable to cry out in pain but first he had to prepare. He ripped off his uniform cap and shirt and jammed them and his gun into the desk drawer. He then went around to Idleman and pushed down on his leg, squeezing blood out of the knife wound.

Vogler took the blood and smeared it all over his undershirt, face and arms, then grabbed one of the knives off the table. He slashed his pants, took a deep breath and dragged the blade across his chest, cutting his shirt and drawing a thin trail of blood.

With time running out, he looked at himself and then at both prisoners and decided his deception was still lacking. He went back to the desk and grabbed the gun by the barrel. He hesitated for a moment then smashed the butt of the gun it into his face. Immediately he could taste the blood and felt his lip swelling. Perfect. He now looked like another poor victim of the Gestapo.

He shoved the gun back into the drawer and grabbed the skinning knife and stood in front of the two Americans. Now all he had to do was kill them and no one would be the wiser.

He was just leaning down to slit Idleman's throat when he heard muffled footsteps right outside the door. With no time to spare, he shoved the knife into his back pocket and collapsed at the Americans' feet.

As he hit the floor, the door burst open. Opening his eyes just enough, Vogler saw three men rush in, all carrying guns. He recognized one of the men as a local he had suspected of working with the Maquis but hadn't yet gotten around to bringing in for questioning. He was a little surprised to see that the other two were American flyers. Could they all possibly be from the same plane?

The thought of having four men from one bomber crew together to interrogate brought a hidden smile—the possibilities were endless.

He needed to act, to distract the Americans before they recognized their friends. "They ran that way," Vogler moaned as he half raised his arm, pointing down the hall.

"Come on!" the Frenchman said, as they headed back out the door. Vogler smiled; all he needed now was just ten seconds to kill the Americans and his deception would be complete.

He had just gotten to his knees when another American rounded the corner and came in. Vogler cursed to himself, he would have to continue to play the part of a beaten prisoner a little longer until he could figure out how to kill the Americans without getting caught.

The young airman rushed over, set his gun on the desk then grabbed Vogler by the arm to help him up. Vogler played his part well, moaning as the American helped him. The German smiled weakly and told his unsuspecting helper that he was all right and he just needed a moment to rest.

Vogler's mind raced. With the American standing guard, there would be no way he could kill the other two unnoticed. He would have to kill him first, kill the other two and hope to make his escape before the others returned.

"I think he is still alive," Vogler said, pointing to Idleman.

Mitchell turned his back to attend to Idleman; as he did, Vogler reached behind him and drew the knife out of his back pocket. He raised it high over his head and was ready to plunge it into the back of the unsuspecting airman when a powerful kick sent the German flipping over the desk.

"What the..." Mitchell said as he spun around.

"He's a Kraut!" Jacobs said.

"Billy?" Mitchell said in amazement.

"He's a Kraut," Jacobs repeated, "an SS Major."

Mitchell grabbed his gun off the desk and pointed it at the German lying on the floor, then called for the others. Moments later Perry, Gibbler, and Franc came rushing into the room

"Look, sir!" Mitchell said excitedly. "It's Billy!"

"And Jerry," Jacobs said, leaning his head toward his still unconscious crewmate.

"I don't believe it!" Perry said as he rushed to untie him while Gibbler attended to Idleman.

While the Americans were tending to their own, Franc stared at the German, who was now standing. "Major Vogler."

"You know him?" Perry asked.

The Frenchman nodded. "Oui. He is in charge of the local Gestapo. A very cruel and ruthless man. He has killed many of my people."

"Did he do this to you?" Perry asked Jacobs.

Jacobs nodded as he rubbed his wrists where the ropes had been. "He would have killed us if you hadn't come along."

"Let's just grease him now and be done with it," Mitchell said, anger and hatred filling his voice.

"I am Major Vogler and as an officer in the German Army, I am formally surrendering to you, Captain, and expect to be treated fairly under the articles of the Geneva Convention as a prisoner of war."

"I don't see any SS major in this room, do you?" Jacobs said.

Perry and the others looked at each other, not sure where Jacobs was going with this. Vogler just frowned. "Come now, Billy, we both know that I am..."

"Not that man!" Jacobs interrupted as he slammed his hands down on the desk. "I see no SS major in here, only someone dressed in civilian clothes, who's behind enemy lines, and since there is no uniform, we have every right to shoot you as a spy."

"We aren't behind enemy lines!" Vogler protested.

Jacobs looked at the four men surrounding him, each carrying a submachine gun.

"Kind of looks that way to me."

"This is ridiculous, my uniform is right here in the desk drawer."

"So, just because there's a uniform in there doesn't make you a major any more than a dress in there would make you a woman."

"What are you thinking here, Billy, a little frontier justice?" Perry asked.

But before the tail gunner could answer, they heard shots coming from outside.

"We've been discovered. We have to get out of here now!" Franc ordered.

"What about him?" Perry asked, tilting his head toward Vogler.

"We'll bring him with us; he may be useful."

Perry glanced at Billy, trying to read his expression, but couldn't tell if he was relieved at not having to make that decision or disappointed.

"Billy, can you walk?" Perry asked.

Jacobs nodded. "I'll be okay."

"Okay, Jeff and I will help Jerry, and you and Mitch keep an eye on our guest here."

"Hurry!" Franc said as he rushed out the door.

Perry and Gibbler each threw one of Jerry's arms over their shoulders and picked him up and headed out the door. Mitchell grabbed Vogler by the arm and shoved him towards the door. Vogler tried to resist but Mitchell shoved him even harder. "Just give me a reason," Mitchell growled as he pointed his gun at the German. Jacobs just sneered at him as he went out the door.

Stepping into the hallway, they saw Franc was already heading up the back stairs, leading a group of three other prisoners they had freed. Perry, Gibbler, and Idleman were close behind.

As they reached the top of the stairs, they could hear the gun battle raging in the street in front of the building. "We've got to hurry before the Germans figure out what's going on and surround the building." Reaching the back door, Franc opened it a crack, then gave the others a thumbs up as he opened it and rushed out.

The cool night air feels so good, Billy thought, stepping out onto the street. He looked up and saw a few patches of stars sparkling between the clouds and had never seen such a beautiful sight; a few minutes ago he thought he would never see another star or anything else ever again.

Suddenly, they heard shouting and three German soldiers rounded the corner. When they didn't stop, the soldiers opened fire. Mitchell spun around and started firing as the others started running. Perry and his group crossed the street and ducked behind a parked car, while Franc tried to hurry his three rescued captives behind a set of stairs leading to another building. Jacobs, Mitchell and Vogler also dashed for cover behind some stairs.

Being battered and beaten, they couldn't move very fast and one of the men was hit, sprawling face first to the ground. Franc shoved his remaining charges behind the stairs and returned fire.

"Get to the car!" Franc shouted to Perry.

"I got him!" Gibbler said as he hoisted Idleman onto his back. "Cover me."

Perry nodded, then leaned around the front of the car and started firing. Gibbler zig-zagged the best he could down the wide sidewalk and quickly ducked around the corner into the alleyway. He nearly slammed Idleman into the car as he stopped and set him down, reaching for the door handle.

"Give me a gun, I can still shoot," Idleman said.

"I've got to get you into the car," Gibbler replied.

Idleman shook his head. "You need all the guns you can get."

Gibbler looked down at his wounded friend and could see the determination in his eyes. "Okay," he said as he took out his .45 and handed it to him. Gibbler pointed to the alley across the street. "Don't let anyone sneak up on us. Got it?" Idleman nodded. "Good, and don't shoot me when I come around the corner either."

Idleman smiled weakly. "No promises, sir. Now go."

Gibbler patted his friend on the back, then raced back to help the others. Because of the gunfire, he couldn't hear the muffled cry of pain from his wounded waist gunner.

"We've got to get to the other side of the street!" Mitchell yelled, ducking down as a piece of the concrete stair railing was torn off by a bullet. Jacobs nodded. "Okay, on the count of three, we shove Fritz here out in front of us and make a dash for the captain."

"What makes you think I'm going to run out in front of you?" Vogler said. "They're shooting at anything that moves."

"Because if you don't move, I'll shoot you right here," Mitchell replied. "And I can't miss from two feet away. At least with them you have a chance."

Jacobs looked at Vogler and could see the anger, frustration, and sense of hopelessness of the situation that filled the German's eyes: it was the same look he wore just moments before. While he didn't revel in the tables now being turned, he did get a great sense of satisfaction that justice was being served by placing the SS major in the exact same position that he had placed so many others before.

"Ready?" Mitchell asked.

Jacobs gave a confident nod.

"Three, two, one... let's go!"

Mitchell grabbed Vogler by the back of the collar and shoved him out in the street while he and Jacobs quickly followed, pointing their guns and firing blindly behind them.

Vogler immediately threw his hands up in the air and started shouting in German not to shoot and that he was a German officer. There was a momentary lull in fire at the strange sight as the German troops tried to figure out what was happening.

Then a single shot rang out and Vogler collapsed to the ground and the fighting resumed. But the lull in fire was enough as Mitchell and Jacobs made it to Perry and the others safely.

"Franc and the other two prisoners are pinned down and there's no way to reach them," Perry said. "We've got to get them out now. It's only a matter of time before reinforcements show up and we're overrun."

"I've got an idea," Gibbler said. "We have two cars. I'll take one and drive it around and park it in front of Franc and his guys, using it as a shield and then you can bring the other car around and pick everyone up."

"Sounds good," Perry answered. "I'll lay down cover fire while you guys get back to the cars, then signal Franc what we're doing."

"Got it, Skipper," Gibbler replied. "Come on guys, let's go."

The crew of the *Red Light Lady* dashed to safety around the corner of the building and were met by gunfire.

"What the hell, Jerry?" Gibbler shouted. "I wasn't kidding earlier about not shooting me."

"I know," Idleman replied calmly. "I also said I could still shoot." He pointed down the alley across the street. "Two Krauts were trying to sneak up on you guys." They all looked across the street and there in the shadows they could see two bodies crumpled against the wall.

"Thanks," Gibbler said. "We have to get out of here now and don't have time to be gentle." He and Mitchell each grabbed an arm and lifted Idleman up and put him in the back seat of the second car. Idleman tried to keep silent but he just couldn't help it as a few yelps of pain escaped his tightly drawn lips.

Moments later they were joined by Perry as he came flying around the corner of the building, chased by a stream of bullets.

"We all set?" the captain asked, catching his breath.

"Ready, Skipper. Jerry and Billy are both in the second car and ready to go. As soon as you and Mitch are ready, I'll go in."

"I'm going with you," Mitchell said.

"Too dangerous," Gibbler replied. "The skipper's gonna need your gun."

"You're gonna need my gun. We've got to keep the Germans' heads down while they pick up the others."

Perry looked at Gibbler. "He's right, Jeff."

Gibbler and Mitchell got into the first car while Perry joined the others in the second.

With a thumbs up from both drivers, Gibbler squealed the tires and disappeared around the corner; five seconds later, Perry followed.

Like a scene from the gangster movie Public Enemy, the two black cars came screeching around the corner, guns blazing. The Germans were momentarily surprised at the assault and took cover as Gibbler's car skidded sideways and ran up onto the stairs that the Frenchman and his charges were hiding behind.

A moment later, Perry brought his car around and spun it sideways, whipping the back end around and "parked" the car against the curb, facing the opposite direction.

Jacobs looked over at his captain with amazement in his eyes. "Wow."

Perry smiled. "My uncle did a little moonshining in his day and taught me how to drive the summer I spent with him when I was 12." Perry smiled. "Mom and Dad still don't know about that."

Jacobs smiled then threw open the door and rushed toward the trapped men. Idleman already had the back door open waiting for the others. Jacobs and Franc dragged one of the men, who had been shot, over to the car and threw him in the backseat. Jacobs started to go back for the other man but Franc grabbed him by the arm and shook his head. Jacobs nodded.

"Okay, get in," he told Franc, then turned and yelled at Gibbler and Mitchell to get into the car.

By now, the Germans had recovered from their surprise and were riddling the car with a heavy barrage of fire, pinning down the two airmen. Perry put the car in reverse and brought it back so fast it slammed into the other car. Mitchell barely had time to jump out of the way before being crushed between the two automobiles.

Everyone jumped in and Perry sent up a plume of smoke as he spun the tires, burning rubber as they left. "Which way?" Perry shouted as they rocketed down the street.

"Left, take a left here," Franc said. "Then a right two blocks down."

"Is everyone okay?" Perry asked, looking over his shoulder.

With a nod from everyone, he turned back around and concentrated on driving. "Good, because we're not out of the woods yet."

As the car sped away, the German soldiers came out and started walking toward the car. A lieutenant and two other troopers walked up to the body of a man lying in the middle of the street.

"I thought I heard him yell out that he was a German officer who had been taken prisoner," one of the soldiers said, looking down on the body.

"Did you?" Lieutenant Schubert sneered. "I didn't hear anything. All I saw was an escaping cretin who needed to be shot."

CHAPTER TWENTY-FOUR

"Where are we going?" Perry asked as they reached the outskirts of the city.

"We have to get you and your men out tonight," Franc said. "We have just, how do you say it, stirred up a hornet's nest. The Germans will stop at nothing now to capture you."

"I'm sorry for all the trouble we've caused," Perry said, "if you want to just dump us off in the woods, I'd understand."

Franc smiled. "I'm not going to dump you in the woods, monsieur. I'm going to throw you into the river."

Perry did a double take and glanced at the backseat at his friends.

"I'm sorry, Captain," Franc said. "I suppose it was a bad joke. My wife says I'm funnier when I don't try to be, I suppose she's right. Are you married, Captain?"

Perry nodded. "Six and a half years."

"Then you know what I am talking about?"

"Indeed I do."

"Anyway, the roads and forests will be heavily patrolled by the Germans looking for your escape to the American lines, so we will move you to safety via the river. It too is guarded, but not as heavily because they do not have the resources to patrol the river as thoroughly. Slow down and take a right at the dirt road there."

Perry slowed the car as they turned onto a road. They drove by several open fields and he thought the road ended but Franc directed him past a broken fence and they were now traveling on what looked more like a beaten path than a road. The grass was overgrown and the tree branches hung down, creating the illusion that they were traveling through a tunnel.

Perry felt like he was going down the rabbit hole from Alice in Wonderland. A sad smile crossed his lips, that was his little girl's favorite story. Would he ever see her again?

"Here we are," Franc said, "pull over to the left."

Perry followed the instructions and was glad that the Frenchman's words snapped him back to the present.

In front of them was an old fishing boat with its bow pulled up onto the shore. From the condition it was in, it looked like sitting on the shore was where it belonged. Even though it was dark, he could see that the paint was chipping and there was dry rot on the cabin. Perry wouldn't have been surprised if the captain came on deck with a peg leg.

Though he had no peg leg, Perry wasn't disappointed when the captain stepped out of the wheelhouse. He looked to be as old as the boat itself. He was short and stocky with a barrel chest, wearing a white, scraggily beard with matching hair. But the feature that struck Perry the most was the captain's eyes. They were set against the backdrop of a tanned, craggy face but instead of being old and weary like the boat, they were bright and youthful.

"This is Capitan..." Franc paused for a moment. "Captain Smith."

Perry chuckled as he reached his hand up. "Thank you, sir, a pleasure to meet you."

The captain smiled as he shook Perry's hand. "Monsieur," he replied with a nod of his head. "But don't thank me yet, you can do that when you are safe behind your own lines."

Perry nodded.

"Come, we have many kilometers to travel."

As soon as everyone was on board, the captain fired up the engines, backed the boat out into the river then pointed the bow downstream.

Jacobs and Idleman were below in the small cabin resting while the other three were in the wheelhouse with Captain Smith.

"Marie," Smith said, affectionately patting the instrument panel, "is old like me, but also like me," pounding his fist against his chest, "she is strong. We have about 50 kilometers to go until we are near the advancing lines. There is much traffic on the river and the Germans are used to seeing many small boats going up and down the river, so they should pay little attention to us.

"The Germans also know me. They are fond of the American whiskey and cigarettes I've been known to smuggle from time to time," he said with a rueful smile. "They tend to ignore me, but who knows after what has happened tonight? But we are running late. I am usually at the drop-off point and headed home while it is still dark, but now we won't arrive until after daylight. I just hope the Germans won't become too suspicious.

"For now, you are free to move about the boat, but if we are spotted, I will show you where you must hide."

"Thank you, Captain Smith."

The captain smiled. "Please, call me André."

The crew of the *Red Light Lady* scattered about the boat to find their own places to sleep, save her captain. Perry found his way to the bow of the small trawler and leaned out over the railing. Flying was his first great love; sailing and being on the water was a close second. He preferred the cry of the gulls and the taste of salt spray from the ocean, but the calm of a river was a good substitute.

"Beautiful, isn't it?" Jacobs said as he joined his captain.

"What... oh, the sunrise," Perry said. "Sorry, I lost track of time."

"Sitting in that chair back at Gestapo headquarters, I never thought I would see another sunrise or sunset again." Perry nodded and for a few moments neither man spoke, then Jacobs continued. "Sir? Am I a bad person?"

Perry looked at his tail gunner. "Why would you say that, Billy?"

"I've always tried to live a good life. I respect others, try to stay out of trouble, I'm no saint, mind you, but..." He hesitated, then continued, "But tonight I wanted to kill a man. The German pilots are shooting and trying to kill us, and we're shooting back and I understand that that's what happens in a war, but tonight was different, it was... well, personal.

"He messed with my mind, sir, and he messed up Jerry real bad. He..." Jacobs barely controlled his emotions. "He made me almost betray my country, sir. He was stabbing Jerry in the legs and was gonna do worse things to him if I didn't tell him what he wanted to know."

Perry put his arm around the young flyer. "You are not a bad person, Billy; in fact, you are one of the most down to earth guys I know. As my grandmother would say, you're the salt of the earth." Jacobs blushed a little as Perry continued. "You wanted to kill him, and that's normal and understandable because of what he did to you and Jerry, but you know what? You didn't. You had the chance to and you didn't take it, and that is what makes you the better man. And as for betraying your country, you were saving a crewmember's life. No, a brother's life. Nothing you could have told him would have made any difference to the war effort, but what you would have said could have saved your brother's life."

"I guess you're right."

"Of course I am. I'm the captain!"

Jacobs smiled. "Yes, sir!"

"Captain Perry!" André shouted from the wheelhouse. "Gather your men quickly, there is a German patrol craft closing in on us from the stern."

Moments later, they were all crowded together in the tiny wheelhouse.

"This is a small boat and I have never smuggled a person before, let alone five! But I have been giving this a great deal of thought, and you must trust me, Captain."

Perry looked at his men, then back to André. "We do."

"Good. Then this is what we must do, and quickly."

André had just lowered his nets into the water when the German patrol boat pulled alongside. It was a heavily armed boat with four heavy machine guns and a forward firing mortar, plus each of her six man crew was armed. André recognized the first officer as he had dealt with him many times in the past, but there was a new captain aboard that he had never seen before. He had a hard, mean look to him, and André suddenly had doubts that they would get out of this alive.

CHAPTER TWENTY-FIVE

"Hello, Erich!" André called out to the first officer. "Good to see you again."

The Frenchman could tell by the troubled look on the first officer's face that he wasn't happy to see him or to even admit that he knew him. Another bad sign.

"I am Lieutenant Pfeiffer and I am in command of this boat," he said sternly, looking at the Frenchman. "You know this man?" He turned his attention back to his first officer.

"Yes, sir. He is a local fisherman..."

"And?"

"And we have had dealings with him in the past. His is known to smuggle contraband, but nothing serious."

"And why has he not been arrested then?"

"Captain Haas considered his small time dealings not worth the effort to investigate any further."

"I am just a simple man trying to make a living and take care of his family," André said, doing his best to sound meek and humble.

"Huh, I'll bet. And what does a simple man like you manage to smuggle?"

"Oh, not much, sir. I come across a bottle of American whiskey or cigarettes from time to time, but that is about all."

"I think you work with the Maquis and you are smuggling resistance fighters!"

"Oh no, monsieur. I don't not smuggle people, only a simple trinket or two."

"Good, then you won't mind us coming aboard to take a look."

André smiled and stepped down from the wheelhouse; he knew the German lieutenant wasn't asking for permission.

"Let's start by having you bring your nets on board."

"But sir, I have only just lowered them over the side, I have not had time to catch any fish yet," André protested.

"Do it now or I will cut the lines and leave them to sink to the bottom."

"Yes, sir," André agreed reluctantly. He went over and attached the line to the boom, then began cranking on the winch, bringing up the nets. As the nets began to rise, one of the German deck hands started shouting and pointing at the nets. Two oblong crates, each about the size of a coffin, began to emerge from the water.

"And what kind of fish do you catch with bait like that?" Pfeiffer said sarcastically, then tipped his head toward the crates, and two of his men jumped onto the fishing boat and began hauling the nets and crates onboard.

"A simple fisherman," Pfeiffer scoffed as he jumped down onto the deck of the fishing boat. "Open it." He nodded to his men who raised their guns.

"I said open it!" he shouted again as the French captain hesitated. Reluctantly, André undid the waterproof latches on the first crate but didn't open it, then undid the latches on the second crate. With a heavy sigh, he opened the lid on the first crate, then the second and stepped back.

"What is this?" Pfeiffer asked. "A trinket or two?"

"As I said, I am just a simple man trying to make a living. This first crate contained an assortment of

German beers and the second contains American beer and British ale."

Before Pfeiffer could say anything, one of the German sailors shouted from below deck. "Captain, I found something."

Pfeiffer glared at André and shoved his way past him as he went below into the small cabin.

"Captain! I found this man hidden under these blankets."

"Who is this? This man looks like he has been beaten and tortured. Another simple trinket you are trying to smuggle"

"Beaten, yes; tortured, no." The Frenchman explained, "And I am not smuggling him. He was under the blankets to keep him warm. He is my wife's cousin and as you can see, he has gotten himself into trouble. My wife was hysterical when she practically threw him onto my boat telling me I had to take him or else they would kill him. There was something about owing certain people money and I'm sure there was a girl involved in there somewhere. I paid little attention to her babblings. I just wanted to get out and go fishing."

Pfeiffer looked at him suspiciously, then turned to his first officer. "Did you search the rest of the boat?"

"Yes, sir, and we have found nothing."

"Very well then, toss the beer over the side and get the men back on board."

"Sir, all of it?" Erich said, almost in a plea. "The men, sir, they would be most grateful..."

The German captain sighed. "Fine, take a couple of bottles apiece for the crew, then dump the rest overboard. But absolutely no drinking on duty!"

"Yes, sir! Thank you, sir!"

Pfeiffer turned back and faced the Frenchman as the rest of his men cleared the boat. "I will be watching you," he said as he poked him in the chest with his finger, "and the trinkets you smuggle."

André let out a huge sigh and felt his knees nearly give way in relief as he watched the German patrol boat pull away and head back upriver. He remained on the stern deck until the patrol boat was a good half mile away before he moved; he did not want to appear too anxious if they were watching him with binoculars. Slowly, he turned and disappeared into the cabin.

"Are you all right?" he said to Idleman.

"Yes, sir, and thank you. Man, that was a close one."

"Very. Now stay here out of sight and I will gather your friends."

André took a quick look on deck and was relieved to see that the German boat had almost disappeared around a bend in the river. Satisfied that they were safe, he rushed down to the engine room.

He approached the first of three 50 gallon fuel drums that were lined up next to the engine and unscrewed the lid. He removed it, then carefully reached in and lifted up a false ten gallon tray of fuel, revealing a dry, hidden compartment underneath.

"Boy, that's a tight squeeze." Perry said as he unfolded himself from the drum. Perry got out and replaced the lid, then helped André free Gibbler and Jacobs from the other two fuel drums.

"Pretty clever having a concealed compartment in a fuel drum," Perry said as he stretched. "I'm sure glad you're on our side."

"Thank you, monsieur. Now if you could help me roll these to the side, we can free your friend."

Each of the airmen grabbed a drum and rolled it off to the side. André took a knife and carefully inserted it between the cracks in boards on the deck and popped out one of the planks. He quickly took out four more boards to reveal Mitchell wedged in between the ribs of the hull.

"That's not fair, sir," Mitchell said as Perry helped him out. "Being the belly gunner, I gotta sit in the bottom of the plane and now I gotta sit in the bottom of the boat too?"

Perry smiled. "At least you got to stretch out. Now we all know what a sardine feels like in a can."

"Please secure the drums," André said. "I'm going back to the wheelhouse and get underway again."

After a few minutes, the Maria was steaming down river again and everyone else was up on the deck, enjoying the fresh air.

"Skipper, I think we got trouble," Gibbler said, pointing upriver.

Perry grabbed the binoculars and looked, then handed them to André.

"We are in trouble," André said. "The German patrol boat is coming back and from the wake on his bow, it looks like he is cruising at full speed."

"Can we outrun him?"

André shook his head. "The Maria is a good boat, but she is not built for speed. We are close to the front line but I don't know if we can reach it in time; it is, how you say, a horse race now."

Just then a huge geyser of water erupted off the starboard side of the stern.

"He is firing his mortar at us!" André said as he shoved the throttles forward.

Perry felt the surge of power but it wasn't the burst of speed he was hoping for.

"He will soon be within gun range," André continued. "I suggest, Captain, that you and your men move up to the bow deck; you will be safer there."

"Do you have anything we can shoot back with?"

The Frenchman shook his head. "I have no weapons to defend ourselves with; being caught with a gun is the same as admitting you are working with the underground to the Germans, so they would not hesitate to shoot me on the spot."

Another geyser erupted, this time to the port side of the stern, followed by several smaller columns of water; they were ranging in with the machine guns.

The five Americans quickly moved to the bow of the boat. "We're in deep trouble here, aren't we, Skipper?" Gibbler said.

Perry nodded. "It doesn't look good, but hey, we've been through worse." Another geyser shot up, this time in front of them.

"We're in range now," Gibbler continued. "Maybe we should surrender?"

"NO!" Jacobs and Idleman shouted almost in unison.

"Sorry, sir," Jacobs said, "but I'm not going back to a room like that. I'm not." He looked over to Idleman, who nodded in support.

"It's settled then; the crew of the *Red Light Lady* will go down fighting."

Between the roar of the engines and the exploding mortar rounds, they didn't hear the faint sound of the planes high overhead that would seal their fate.

CHAPTER TWENTY-SIX

"Colonel, 10 o'clock low, river traffic. It looks like a German patrol boat is chasing a fishing vessel. I count three to four guns on the German, the civilian looks unarmed."

Colonel Adams squinted, looking at the German boat: how could his wingman see those guns from way up here? Oh to have young eyes again, he thought.

"Whoa, those guys have a mortar down there. They almost plastered the fishing boat that time. Colonel?"

"Doc, you and Andy stay high and take top cover, the lieutenant and I will strafe the Germans," Colonel Wesley Adams ordered.

"Roger."

The two North American P-51 Mustangs pulled up a little and circled high above the river, keeping a watchful eye over their sister ships while they started their dive toward the water. The early morning sun blazed off the polished aluminum skins of the two other fighters, making them look like bolts of lightning as they streaked earthward.

"Follow me in trail, about 400 yards back," Adams said. "I want to make this in just one pass."

"Right behind you, sir," replied his wingman, Lieutenant Luke Stevens. Stevens cut his throttle as he fell in line behind his lead. He loved the challenge of aerial combat, pushing his machine and himself to the limits, but there was just something about ground attacks that he loved.

In the air, even though planes were flying past each other at hundreds of miles an hour, it was hard to get a sense of speed; but ground attack was different. Diving down and skimming only a few feet above the earth with the trees and buildings being nothing more than a blur as he went streaking by was such a kick. At 21, he still found it hard to believe at times that they were actually paying him to do stuff like this.

Stevens followed as the colonel approached the gunboat. He had swung around and was approaching them low from behind, coming in out of the rising sun. Having been the colonel's wingman for 22 missions, he knew the colonel would have preferred a high attack angle, making it harder for the German gunners to get a bead on them, but having the sun at your back was worth the greater risk.

Stevens was behind and slightly above Adams as he fired. Two parallel columns of water shot up behind the German gunboat in its wake. He watched as bullets from the six .50 caliber guns threw up chunks of metal and wood as they tore into the stern of the boat.

Smoke began pouring out of the engine room and a small fire started as ammo from one of the machine guns exploded. Adams streaked passed the gunboat, barely missing its antenna, then pulled up and banked to the right.

Now it was Stevens' turn.

He came in at a little bit higher angle than his lead, giving him a couple of extra seconds on target. He squeezed the trigger and saw his tracer shells pour into the boat. The mast fell like a chopped tree, and smoke and fire now gushed out of the stern.

Just as he flew over the boat, Stevens looked back and saw it explode. "Hee Haw! Did you see that, sir?" Stevens called excitedly over the radio. But his joy and excitement were short lived as he looked forward just in time to see the fishing boat explode and the stern flip over; the Germans had gotten off one more mortar round before they were sunk.

CHAPTER TWENTY-SEVEN

The ringing in his ears was louder than the bells at St. Patrick's Cathedral and his head throbbed, pounding out a new sensation of pain with each beat of his heart. He tried to open his eyes but the light hurt. Even when his eyes had adjusted to the light, his vision was still blurry.

He tried to focus but was having a great deal of difficulty. He saw a splash of color on the wall in front of him and he tried to focus on it. He could see that it was red and couldn't tell if something was on it, then realized that it must be the Nazi flag.

Immediately he fell into despair. The fact that he was still alive held very little consolation for him: he was now a Prisoner of War.

"Captain Perry, can you hear me?" Perry groaned and turned his head. He could see the blurred image of a nurse smiling at him. "Good, you're awake, I'll get the doctor." Then she turned and left.

A moment later, a man wearing a white lab coat walked in. "Nice to have you back. You gave us quite a scare."

"You speak pretty good English," Perry muttered. "Not much of an accent at all."

The doctor and nurse looked at each other, puzzled by their patient's strange remark, then the doctor smiled.

"Captain Perry, just where do you think you are?"

"From that flag over there, I'd say I'm a guest of the Fatherland." Perry flopped his arm in the general direction of the flag.

"How's your vision? Is it a little blurry?"

"Yeah."

"I want you to look around, Captain. I want you to concentrate on your surroundings, then tell me what you see."

Perry sighed, not sure what kind of game they were playing, but he did as he was told anyway. He began looking around the room and was surprised. He wasn't in a regular hospital ward with pale walls and pale curtains—no, he was in a single large room that was dark, except for one side that seemed to be lined with windows.

Slowly his eyes began to focus. He could now make out details; he could see that the walls were dark, not because they were painted but because they were lined with books, hundreds and hundreds of books, and the Nazi flag wasn't a flag at all, but a large tapestry. It was red, but instead of the swastika in the middle there was an ornate design.

"You are not the guest of the Fatherland, Captain; you are the guest of the French people and Uncle Sam."

"You mean I'm not a prisoner?" Perry asked, still not quite believing.

"No, you are not a prisoner. We fished you out of the water on the American side of the river. You are a free man, Captain."

Perry smiled and let out a huge sigh of relief, but his smile quickly faded and was replaced with concern. "My crew, what happened to my crew?"

"They're fine, Captain, they are all just fine."

"What happened?"

"Two Mustangs strafed and sank the gunboat, but it managed to get off one more mortar round that hit your vessel in the stern. The boat exploded and flipped over. You and your men are extremely lucky to be alive."

"What about André?"

"I'm afraid he didn't make it."

Just then Gibbler came hobbling up on crutches, followed by Jacobs pushing Idleman in a wheelchair.

"Hey, Skipper, good to see your lazy butt finally awake... sir!" Gibbler smiled.

"Jeff, Billy, Jerry, am I ever glad to see you guys," Perry said as they gathered around his bed. "Where's Mitchell?"

"He's in traction in another ward," Jacobs said, "but the doctors say he'll be just fine."

"So what's the story, Doc, now that Sleeping Beauty is awake?" Gibbler asked.

"We'll keep all of you for a few more days until you're ready to travel, then we'll ship you all home."

"I hope those guys back at base haven't gone through all of our stuff and cleared out our hut." Jacobs said.

The doctor smiled. "When I say you're going home, I don't mean England. I mean back to the States, the good ol' U.S. of A."

"What?" they all said in unison.

The doctor smiled again. "That's right, I said we're sending you back to the States."

"I can't believe it," Jacobs said. "We're going home."

CHAPTER TWENTY-EIGHT

December 31, 1945: Empire State Building

The music was loud and the dance floor was crowded. People were celebrating. They were celebrating a new year, celebrating the end of the war, celebrating the promise of a new beginning.

Billy Jacobs, Jerry Idleman, and Tommy Svensen were sitting at their table, drinks in hand, watching what was happening on the dance floor.

"My, how the mighty have fallen," Idleman said, pointing to Tony Ramos.

"I know," Jacobs replied. "Tony's been spending an awful lot of time with her."

"Do you think he's in love?" Svensen asked.

Jacobs shook his head. "I don't know, only time will tell, but I do know that they are," he said, pointing at their captain. "They haven't taken their eyes off of each other all night. Just look at them, that my friend is what it's all about."

"You sound jealous," Idleman jibed.

"I wouldn't mind finding a nice girl to settle down with."

"Never happen."

"And why not?" Jacobs shot back.

"Because you're too ugly, that's why," Idleman laughed.

"Shut up!" Jacobs said, shoving his former crewmate.

"You shut up," Idleman retorted.

"Both of you shut up," Svensen interrupted. "Where's the lieutenant?"

"He's at the bar. He ran into a couple of guys from the squadron and is over there telling stories and swapping lies," Jacobs replied.

"How 'bout Mitchell? I've barely seen him all night and it's almost time for the toast."

"There he is," Jacobs said, pointing through the crowd to the balcony. "He's been playing tour guide for the last couple of days."

Mark Mitchell was on the balcony pointing out the sights of the big city to René and his wife Claire, the farm couple who had helped him, Captain Perry, and Lieutenant Gibbler escape. And standing by their side was their son Louis. True to his word, Perry was able track down their son, who had survived Dunkirk and had served with the Free French during the war. Perry was able to have him flown back home after the war ended.

When the music stopped, Jacobs stood and waved for Mitchell and the others to come back in. Excitement was in the air as the crowd started the countdown toward the New Year. But all those who were gathered around the table in the back corner were in a world all their own.

Everyone took their seats but when Perry took his glass and began to stand for the toast, René put his hand on Perry's shoulder and held him down as he, his wife and son stood.

"We are honored to be here with you, Captain," René said. "But this is between you and your men." Perry started to reply, but René stopped him. "You forget, monsieur, that I too served my country and understand the bond that is forged between men in battle. Thank you, but this is your time… it is their time." Perry nodded in gratitude as the three of them stood and moved quietly behind them.

"Gentlemen, a toast," Perry said as he stood and raised his glass.

The men stood solemnly and raised their glasses as Perry spoke.

"To the *Red Light Lady*, may she always find fair skies."

"Here, here," the men replied in unison as they clinked their glasses and took a sip.

"And here's to the men who flew her, best damned crew in the 8th Army Air Force," Perry said, looking each man in the eye.

Another round of clinking and drinking.

"And here's to those who have gone before."

The table they were at had been set for thirteen, the seven members of the crew plus three for René and his family. But all eyes now were focused on the three additional empty place settings.

"To Joe Thomas," Perry said.

"To Joe Thomas," they echoed.

"To Charlie Tasker."

"To Charlie Tasker.

"To Eric Blocker."

"Eric Blocker."

By now the countdown was over; it was officially 1946. The falling confetti and dropping balloons pulled them out of their moment of silence, back to reality, to life – and to honor those lives by not only honoring their memory, but by living their own.

With the band playing Auld Lang Syne, they all gathered around the table together. Mike Perry showing off pictures of his daughter, Tony Ramos being teased by his friends warning his girlfriend what a scallywag he was. René and his family talking of the marvels of the big city and wondering how they could ever go back to their tiny village after this.

They were celebrating the start of a new year, celebrating the end of the war, celebrating a new beginning.

THE END

CONTINUE READING FOR A SAMPLE OF

A WORLD WAR II THRILLER BY PAUL BYERS. AVAILABLE NOW!

ONE

THE car drifted slowly to a stop with its engine and lights off.

The driver hesitated for a moment, his eyes darting back and forth, surveying the area for any hidden dangers that might be lurking in the shadows. He knew this had been planned out to the last detail, but even with the best-laid plans, things could go wrong. A cold shudder traveled the length of his spine because he knew what the deadly consequences would be if this plan went wrong. He took a deep breath to calm his fears, pushed his glasses up off the bridge of his nose, and opened the door. Even before his feet touched the ground, two figures emerged out of the darkness and moved toward him like specters.

Both men were dressed in military uniforms, but in the dim, pre-dawn darkness, he couldn't tell if they were American, British, or German. The taller of the two phantoms spoke as he held out his hand. "Good morning, Doctor Strovinski. If ya'll just step this way, we'll have you outta here and back in England in no time at all."

As soon as the soldier spoke, Strovinski knew: American. He hated the way the Americans had butchered the English language with their slang, but this American was even worse. He had a . . . what did they call it? A Southern drawl? He thought the man sounded like one of those cowboys from their shoot'em-up western movies.

Doctor Nicoli Strovinski was on the high side of his fifties with thinning brown hair, and his large waistline reflected the fact that he was a man dedicated to science and little else. "Let's be quick about this," he said in Russian. Let the Cowboy try and figure that one out.

The Cowboy replied politely in perfect Russian, "Right this way, sir."

So what? Strovinski thought. The cowboy can understand and speak Russian.

He followed behind them in silence, clutching his worn leather briefcase. The night air was cool and clear, washed clean by heavy rains earlier in the day.

In the stillness of the night, their shoes crunched against the gravel, sounding like a column of marching soldiers rather than just three men walking. They rounded the corner of a small building that he guessed to be a barn because of the foul animal odors coming from inside. Strovinski stopped dead in his tracks. It was a peculiar sight to see two fighters and a bomber parked behind the barn. But it was an even stranger thing to see a cow grazing peacefully under the left wing of the bomber and a goat rubbing its head against the propeller of one of the smaller planes. These cowboys must be smarter than he gave them credit for, he thought, getting three Allied aircraft this deep behind enemy lines.

Strovinski was a little disappointed with the small two-engine plane that was taking him out of Germany. He had expected to be whisked away by one of their big B-17 bombers. Although he didn't know much about American aircraft, everyone in France and Germany knew what the Flying Fortress looked like. After nearly three years of seeing the big plane dominate the skies over France and Germany, it had become the symbol of the advancing Allied forces. To those in France, it represented their impending liberation; to the German Army, it represented impending defeat. For Strovinski, perhaps it would mean a new life.

He followed the two cowboys around to the back of the plane and watched the shorter one climb up a small ladder and disappear into the black abyss. The taller cowboy motioned for Strovinski to follow. Drawing a deep breath, he realized that this was no longer a dream but that it was really happening. There was no turning back now as his foot came to rest on the first rung of the ladder.

He froze in mid-step, a cry of terror on his lips, as another apparition appeared from the black void in the form of a disembodied hand that reached out to grab him. The phantom materialized into a round, baby-faced crewman who was reaching out to help him up the ladder. The blond young ghost looked to be only eighteen or nineteen years old, barely old enough to wear long pants, let alone fight in a war. He wondered if he had made the right decision.

The young man reached out to take his briefcase, but Strovinski refused to give it up. It contained the culmination of nearly twenty years of work and he wasn't about to trust it to a child who didn't know the meaning of life. Not even for a second while he boarded the plane. Grunting, and feeling a little foolish for letting his vivid imagination get the better of him, Strovinski managed to hoist himself up through the small hatchway with one hand. Once inside, he let the boy lead him through the bowels of the plane.

He thought that a bomber by its very nature should be big and spacious, but reality proved him wrong. He struck his head twice on the short trip from the hatch to his seat. He quickly sat down and nervously fastened his seat belt.

The plane had a dusty and oily smell to it. He could also smell the telltale odor of gunpowder, sweat, and something else . . . Was it the faintest trace of fear that mingled with the other aromas? But was it the plane crew's fear or his? His stomach answered his brain's question by rumbling and reminding him of just how much he hated flying.

"GOLDILOCKS, Papa Bear, Mama Bear, and Baby Bear are ready for takeoff."

Captain Jack Lofton of the Royal Air Force, or RAF, shook his head at the radio message from the bomber as he flipped on the ignition switch to his Supermarine Spitfire, waking up his sleeping warhorse. The bloody Yanks and their silly code words, he thought. When he'd been asked to volunteer for a joint U.S.-British mission, he immediately agreed; but he'd signed on to fight the Germans, not recite nursery rhymes. He was "Mama Bear," and his wingman, Lieutenant Reginald "Reggie" Smyth, was "Baby Bear." What next? he thought. If they got in trouble over the channel, were they to land on the Good Ship Lollypop?

At twenty-six, Lofton had a soft, youthful smile and bright blue eyes that were in contrast to the premature weariness which now fit him like his uniform. He had been barely more than a boy when he'd joined the RAF, but after nearly five years of fighting he appeared to be the age of a man ten years his senior.

He looked over to Reggie, whom he imagined wore a grin from ear to ear, eager for the adventure to begin. A sad smile crossed his lips as he shook his head. He wondered if he'd ever been that young. With one last good tug on his harness, he signaled Baby Bear to take off.

The fast, steady rhythm of the British Rolls-Royce Merlin fighter engines joined the loping sound of the twin Pratt & Whitney eighteen-cylinder radial engines of the American's Martin Marauder B-26. They combined for a mechanical harmony that reached a pitched crescendo when full throttle was applied.

"Papa Bear to Goldilocks, Papa Bear to Goldilocks: the package is in the basket and we are on our way home."

CAPTAIN Griffin Avery of the Office of Strategic Services, or OSS, took off his headset and dropped it on the table. He let out a sigh of relief and rubbed the back of his neck. He pushed himself away from the table that held a fifteen-hour collection of cigarette butts, empty coffee cups, and several stale, half-eaten sandwiches and doughnuts. It had been a very long day and night.

From his basement office in a nameless government building in London, he had monitored the flight of the Three Bears and their pick up of Dr. Nicoli Strovinski. He had watched them since they'd left England in the pre-dawn hours, followed them across the English Channel and over occupied France. Now at last, they were on their way home.

Avery stood and stretched. At forty-five, his hair was already turning gray, but he took comfort in the fact that he at least still had all his hair—unlike his father, who was bald on top with only a fringe of hair running around the side of his head. He preferred to think that his graying temples gave him the distinguished look of a gentleman and not that of an old man.

He heard sharp, fast-paced footsteps coming down the hall and wondered who could be coming here at this late hour. The door opened and Avery sprang to attention. "Good evening, General," he barked with as much enthusiasm as he could muster.

"At ease," came the reply. At sixty-two, Brigadier General Arthur Sizemore carried himself like a man half his age. He was a short, barrel-chested man with the personality and face of a bulldog that liked to chase parked cars. Like his height, his demeanor was short and direct.

"Got a hot date, sir?" Avery asked, seeing his boss was wearing his dress uniform. Immediately Avery cringed, regretting his choice of words. *Got a date?* What was he thinking?

Sizemore ignored Avery's feeble attempt at humor and surveyed the messy desk. He scrutinized the room like a father visiting his son's college dorm room for the first time and not liking what he saw. "My 'date' is with the chiefs of staff at a late-running state dinner—a damn waste of time, if you ask me," Sizemore replied, plucking at his collar that vanity wouldn't allow him to admit was two sizes too small. "This is the fourth scientist this month we've nabbed. Who is this guy again?"

"Doctor Nicoli Strovinski, one of Germany's top nuclear physicists. It's been suspected that for the last year or so he's been working closely with Werner Heisenberg, head of the Nazi atomic program. He's also known in the academic community for his work in quantum mechanics and—"

"Right, he's some sort of hotshot egghead. Didn't he also work with Von Braun at Peenemunde on the V-2s?"

"Yes sir, that's why we decided to grab him. If Germany could develop some sort of atomic weapon with the V-2 as the delivery system, then they could hold the world for ransom. We have no defense against a V-2."

"Man, I'd love to tell Ike that we bagged this boy." Sizemore paused then grunted, his face even more serious than usual. "If he's so damn important, you'd better not screw this up. And remember, Captain"—he pointed his stubby finger in Avery's face—"it may be my butt, but it's your neck on the line here." Sizemore turned to leave and stopped when he reached the door. "And clean this mess up." He tugged at his collar again and disappeared.

As the door slammed shut, Avery collapsed in his chair. He wasn't sure if he was more relieved that the mission was almost over or that Sizemore was gone. He grabbed a pack of cigarettes out of his front pocket and lit one with his Ronson. Avery leaned back, took a deep drag, and put his headset back on. He would continue to monitor the flight until they were halfway over the channel. Only then would he relax and go to the airfield to collect the doctor.

Avery began foraging through the scattered doughnuts on his desk, searching for one that wasn't stale enough to use as a doorstop. He found an edible morsel buried amongst the greasy rubble and held it up as if he had discovered a nugget of gold, a look of triumph filling his face. He took a bite and sighed. It wasn't the freshest he'd ever had; if only he had some fresh coffee. He was devouring the last bite when the radio crackled to life.

"Break left Baby Bear, Baby . . . oh, bloody hell, Reg! Break left!" the voice on the radio shouted. "You've got two bandits behind you!"

Avery sprang up and checked the channel on his radio.

"Bloody good, lad," the radio blared again. It was the voice of Captain Lofton, and it sounded like they were under attack. Avery heard the roar of the airplane engine and the unmistakable sound of machine guns firing. How can this be, Avery wondered. How could the Germans have known about Strovinski?

"Goldilocks, Goldilocks, this is Papa Bear. We are under fighter attack! I say again, we are under attack. Mama Bear and Baby Bear have engaged."

The sound of the bombers' distress call shook Avery out of his stupor and he grabbed the microphone. "Papa Bear, this is Goldilocks, do you copy? Where are you? Do you copy? *Answer me!* Papa Bear this is Goldilocks, do you read me? Mama Bear, do you read me, over?"

"Breaking left. I'm going to flip over and bring him back in front of you," Smyth replied. Avery could hear and almost feel the tension in the young British pilot's voice

"Roger, swinging around now to line up." By contrast, Avery could hear the calm voice of the seasoned Lofton over the drone of his engine.

"You've got two more coming down on you, Reg, eight o'clock high!"

"I can't see them. I can't see them!" Smyth shouted desperately in the radio.

"They're right above the bomber, swing back to your left, behind the bomber, NOW!"

His mission was falling apart, yet Avery could only listen with morbid fascination as the battle unfolded before him. He was reminded of Halloween night back in 1938. He was home on leave and had just come back from the corner grocer. His mom had wanted fresh corn on the cob to serve with their steak in celebration of the return of their long-gone son.

When he walked through the front door, he found his mother hysterical, glued to the radio. She kept shouting about being under attack. He dropped the bag of groceries on the table and rushed to the front room. On the radio, the reporter was saying something about people being killed and that the Army was on the scene but the enemy had some sort of new weapon, some sort of death ray.

Avery could hear yelling and screaming in the background and something that sounded like gunfire. The reporter shouted that they were under attack, and then there was silence.

His mother was on the verge of crying, and his father just sat there and held her, not knowing what to do. Avery was reaching for the phone to call headquarters when the radio came back to life and the announcer said that he hoped they were enjoying the broadcast of Orson Welles and his Mercury Theater production of *War of the Worlds*. It took some convincing, but his mother finally realized that it was just a radio show and not the end of the world. Upon pain of death, she threatened him and his father against saying a word to anyone that she had believed the broadcast.

Now Avery sat and listened as his own radio played out its own scene. Only this time, the sound effects weren't made in a studio and those weren't actors. Real people were going to die.

"My left aileron's hit, I can hardly turn!"

Avery could hear the rising fear in Lieutenant Smyth's voice.

"Steady, lad," Lofton calmly responded over the radio. "I'm almost there."

Then silence.

Avery leaned forward in his chair as if that could help him hear better, but there was nothing to hear. The only sound was the pounding of his heart. "*This is Goldilocks! Does anybody read me*?" he yelled in frustration shaking the microphone as if he could bully it into working. Why won't this damn thing work? "Jack! Do you copy? He broke the rules by using Lofton's name, but he didn't care. "Jack, where are you?"

Silence.

Avery was resigning himself to the fact that the entire mission had failed and eight lives were lost, when the radio blared again.

"What the bloody hell! Is that a red star? *REGGIE*!" Even through the roar of the fighter's engine, Avery could hear a faint explosion and he knew that Smyth was gone. Sitting in his warm and comfortable office, it was hard for him to comprehend that he had just heard a man die.

Avery sat like a statue, his chest barely moving as he breathed, a thousand thoughts bounced around in his head.

"Papa Bear, this is Mama Bear. Do you copy? Papa Bear, this is Mama Bear. Do you read me? Over." Slowly, like the incoming tide, Avery felt hope creeping back into his soul as he heard Lofton's voice on the radio. Perhaps Lofton had fended off the attackers and Strovinski was safe.

But the incoming tide quickly turned into a tidal wave as the radio blasted another warning: "Break right, Mama Bear, break right!"

"Look out, Mama Bear, there's another one coming down on you! Break! Goldilocks, Goldilocks, this is Papa Bear. Mama and Baby Bear are both down, repeat, both fighters are down! Am under heavy fire. Wait . . . top gunner! Watch that one coming down, nine o'clock high! He's in behind us, swing it around *now*! Tail gunner report! Report! Goldilocks we have—"

Silence: total, deafening silence now invaded his office. It smothered the room like a thick heavy fog, driving everything else out, all thoughts of reason, any lingering feelings of hope and, oddly, even of despair. The silence was so consuming that Avery found it difficult to breathe.

What had gone wrong?

Avery placed his elbows on the table and buried his head in his hands, trying to think. After a moment he leaned back and ran his fingers through his hair and noticed a small mustard and mayonnaise stain on his sleeve. His desk that looked like a high school cafeteria. He shook his head and sighed. Given the way the room looked, his stupid date joke and stains on his uniform, it was no wonder General Sizemore didn't have much confidence in him.

But Sizemore was wrong! He'd planned everything, down to the last detail. It had taken him three weeks to go through each phase, step by step, and to finalize everything into a complete plan. He'd checked and rechecked it all at least a dozen times. Each of his two assistants had gone over it with a fine-tooth comb to see if they could find any flaws. And there had been none. He'd seen to the security precautions personally to prevent this very thing.

He didn't know how long he sat there, seconds, minutes, hours; it didn't matter. He fumbled mindlessly with a cigarette and burned his fingers before he realized that it was already lit. What had gone wrong? They should have been in and out before the Germans had even realized that Strovinski was missing, yet they had known and had been waiting . . . but was it the Germans? Something that Captain Lofton had said over the radio, something about a red star. The only aircraft he knew that carried a red star were Russian. In the dark of night and heat of battle had Lofton confused the swastika for a star? Not likely. He doubted that a man with his experience would make such a mistake.

Even though the Americans, British, and Russians were all allies, as they pushed further and further into Germany, it was becoming a race with the British and Americans against the Russians in an effort to capture German technology and resources. Did the Russians somehow find out about their plan and shoot Strovinski down themselves, Avery wondered, rather than let the Americans have him? Or was it just a case of blind luck? Had the Germans just been in the right place at the right time and stumbled across the three allied planes?

It didn't matter now. They were all dead and it was his fault.

Avery stood and tilted his head from side to side, trying to get the kinks out of his neck. His mind was as numb as his body. He couldn't think straight. He needed to get some fresh air. This was the first mission in which he'd been directly responsible for the deaths of those under him. He'd sent men and women into France before to help the resistance and he'd found out later that some had been captured and even killed, but this was different. The Three Bears and Strovinski were dead because *his* plan had failed!

He grabbed his coat and wandered down the hallway, ignoring the few early birds arriving to work, then climbed the stone staircase up two flights to the street above. Wearily, he leaned against the heavy wooden door and summoned all his remaining strength to push it open. Avery squinted his eyes as he stepped out into the street. It was one of those rare, bright sunny mornings in London.

Across the street was a small tailor shop with a bouquet of colorful flowers in the window, a splash of color that seemed so out of place in war-weary London. Half a block down there had been a little family-owned bakery. They made the best glazed doughnuts he had ever tasted. Each time he went in there, the sights and aromas took him back to his once-a-month family trips into the city when he was a boy. On the first Saturday of each month, providing his father didn't have to work, he and his brother would ride in the back of their old Ford Model T as it rambled and rumbled down the dirt road twelve miles into Portland, Oregon. His mother said that his eyes always grew to the size of the doughnuts themselves as he gazed upon row after row of the delectable delights. And the aroma . . . the warm, soft smells of the flour and butter baking made it an almost magical experience.

Sometimes when he felt homesick, he had gone into the British bakery just to remember; his own little personal escape from the war. Yesterday, before all this had started, he had stopped in and bought half a dozen.

Sometime during the night, he had heard the rumblings and felt the impact of what he guessed was a V-2 rocket that had slammed into the ground nearby, shaking his old building to its cornerstone. The V-2s were Hitler's *Vergeltungswaffen,* or Vengeance Weapons. It was a 46-foot-high, 3500-mile-per-hour monster designed for pure terror. They weren't extremely accurate, but by carrying over a ton of explosives, they didn't have to be.

Today, the bakery was a burned out crumpled ruin. It must have taken a direct hit last night. How ironic, he thought, that yesterday, like the bakery, he had been busy and full of life and hope for the future. Now, both the street and his spirit were a pile of broken dreams and rubble.

TWO

THE laughter was loud, drowning out conversation, music, and tonight, even the war. At the far corner of the bar sat an old man known to everyone simply as The Colonel. He was in good shape for a man of 81, too old to fight but not too old to proudly serve his country in the Home Guard, ready to rout the Huns if they dared to stick their noses across the channel. The Colonel had flaming white hair, a large handlebar mustache, and a passion for life still burned deep in his bright, clear eyes. His skin was a tough and leathery brown, reflecting decades of service for king and country.

Tonight, like most every night, he sat at the bar, reliving the glory days of his youth to whoever would listen. He often spoke fondly of the lads of the 24th Regiment of Foot and those fateful days in South Africa at Rorke's Drift in 1879—the time of the great Zulu uprising.

He reminisced about how he was just a lad, only fifteen at the time, and of how he had run away from home seeking adventure. He could think of nothing more exciting than camping out all the time, so he lied about his age and joined the army. He would describe the smashing old uniforms—how good they all looked in their bright red coats, white helmets, and bandoliers! He recounted how he and the lads had stood toe to toe with nearly four thousand Zulu savages and held them at bay.

One day, Avery remembered, a drunk British sailor had called The Colonel a liar and said he had never been in Africa or fought against the Zulu. The Colonel was silent for a moment then slowly stood and unbuttoned the top two buttons of his tunic. With great care and reverence he pulled out a Victoria Cross that hung from a tarnished chain around his neck.

"Twelve medals were awarded that day," The Colonel said slowly, "but only eleven officially. It was the most ever issued to a unit for a single engagement. When the army found out that I was really only fifteen, they couldn't acknowledge that they had let a boy fight, so they let me keep the medal but made me swear never to reveal my true age at the time."

After that, no one ever questioned The Colonel again.

SITTING at a table, Avery noticed, off to one side, was a group of women—girls, really—from RAF headquarters. They were with the Fighter Command. Some had helped direct the magnificent Spitfires and Hurricanes which had fended off the Luftwaffe in the dark days surrounding the Battle of Britain. They were young and pretty, but several, those who had been around since the beginning, had a few more worry lines and a few more gray hairs than the newer girls. They were seasoned veterans at the ages of twenty-three and twenty-four. Few people knew of the hard work they did or just how close the Germans had actually come to winning the battle and invading England.

There were several small groups of British and American soldiers scattered throughout the bar, telling tall tales and swapping lies in hopes of impressing the local girls. There were also a few civilians about doing their best to set aside the war for a moment. But most of the patrons that night were American airmen. It was easy to tell the bomber crews from the fighter pilots, Avery thought. The fighter pilots usually flocked in groups of three to four, while the bomber crews stuck together in packs of seven or eight.

At the far end of the bar were four flyboys, fighter pilots. One gestured with his hands, describing in great detail his latest aerial victory. In the back of the pub sat a group of eight flyers surrounding two empty chairs. They were much quieter than the rest of the patrons as they raised their glasses in a silent toast, a scene that was often repeated. They were a bomber crew who had lost two of their own and were now saying goodbye. Next to them was an empty table with ten chairs stacked on top of it. The crew that didn't come back must have been well known and liked, Avery thought, for the pub to hold a table in tribute to them on such a crowded night.

Captain Avery sat in the back of the pub taking it all in. It had been two days since his report on the loss of Dr. Strovinski, and General Sizemore had not been pleased. He'd had dreams of moving "upstairs" and working with the big boys on major planning projects. But with the war winding down in Europe, his chances of being transferred to the Pacific and being involved with the invasion of Japan were all but gone now with the loss of Strovinski.

His less-than-glamorous nine-to-five job involved working with the resistance cells in France, gathering information about German troop movements, and aiding the recovery of downed Allied pilots. With the rapidly advancing Allied forces, he'd also been assigned the task of locating top German scientists and grabbing them before the Russians did.

With certain technologies, the Germans held a slight edge. In some cases, however, their advantage was monumental. Though the British had a jet powered fighter in the Gloster Meteor, it was no match for the German Messerschmitt 262 . . . and the Allies had nothing to counter the dreaded V-2 rockets. While Russia was an ally, the United States and Britain still wanted to make sure that they were in control of these new technologies. It was Avery's job to get the scientists, a job he had now failed at miserably.

Avery took another sip of his beer—or his pint, as the Brits called it. It was his third, and he was nearing that place where he felt no pain, a place that suited him just fine.

The Three Bears had been his plan. His operation from start to finish. It was supposed to show General Sizemore that he could do more than just pass messages back and forth between headquarters and the resistance. It was to prove that he belonged upstairs with the big boys.

But none of that mattered now.

He'd gotten good men killed. In three large gulps, he downed the rest of his beer and waved his hand at the waitress for another.

"Griff, my boy, why the look of a man who's just found out his mother-in-law is coming to live with him?"

Avery looked up from his empty glass and watched The Colonel spin the chair around and sit backwards in it, holding his beer in one hand and leaning forward on the back of the chair with the other.

"Do you know what I had to do today, Colonel? I had to write letters to the families of the men I lost on a mission . . . a mission that I planned. I planned it down to the last detail, but somehow it went horribly wrong. I knew one of the men personally. I even ate with him and his family. He had a wife and two little girls, four and six. We don't even have a body to give back to her to lay to rest. She has no grave to cry over, only this lousy piece of paper saying her husband was a hero and is missing in action. For God's sake, I can't even tell her what happened to him or where he went down. They died for nothing."

The warmth and humor in the old man's eyes drained. "We were in France," The Colonel began, "in the early spring of 1916 during the war that was supposed to end all wars. The nights were still cold, as Mother Nature still hadn't taken off her winter coat yet, and the rains that April were unusually heavy, turning our trenches and the no-mans land into a sea of mud, muck, and mire."

A humorless smile slowly crossed The Colonel's lips. "It's funny what you remember, but what I remember most, other than my lads, was the smell. The rich, earthy smell of the soil was invaded by the musty stench of everything rotting and covered in mold from the continual rains.

"We'd been stalemated for most of the month, neither us nor the Huns taking more than a few yards of ground at a time, when some general back at headquarters decided that he wanted the stalemate broken.

"Our platoon was handed the nasty assignment of taking out a German machine-gun bunker on a slight rise that controlled nearly the entire line in our area. If we were to advance at all, those guns had to be destroyed." The Colonel paused and closed his eyes for a moment. Avery couldn't tell if he was trying to remember or trying to forget what happened that day.

"It was particularly cold that morning," he resumed, "and a thin layer of ice covered the mud. We were all cold so were stomping our feet to keep warm, and with each stomp of our boots, you could hear the crunching of the ice breaking. I think that the Germans must have heard the crunching and knew something was up because they were waiting for us.

"When the whistle blew, we all charged up over the top of the trench with our best war cries . . . straight into the teeth of hell. The war cries instantly turned in to screams of agony as the Kraut machine guns opened up on our boys.

"Johnny Biggelow was a scrawny mutt of a lad, but what he didn't have in size he made up for in heart. He was the first one over the top, and the first to die. His foot hadn't even cleared the top of the trench when he was hit. He was blown back and landed on top of me, and we both went tumbling down into the mud. He probably saved my life, because the whole first wave was wracked by machine-gun fire. I'll never forget the emptiness of his eyes as they stared back at me."

The Colonel paused.

"We eventually took those machine gun nests that day, but I lost three quarters of my squad. Three days later, we abandoned that field and the Germans moved right back in. It was my whistle that sent my lads over the top, my orders that got them killed. And just like you I had to write letters home to their loved ones. And to this day I remember each and every one of them. Did they die for nothing?" The old man silently shook his head. "No, they sacrificed themselves serving their country and serving their brothers; they died doing their duty and so did your lads. Don't take that away from them. If you forget that, then their deaths truly have no meaning."

"I guess you're right," Avery said. "I was feeling pretty sorry for myself and that's not what it's about."

"Good! Just remember the lads and their death won't be in vain." The Colonel raised his glass in a toast and Avery followed suit. "To our boys!" He said as their glasses came together. Both men drank, and Avery put his glass down, still distracted. The Colonel followed the gaze of his American friend until it stopped on a table across the room.

A smile reclaimed its rightful place on the old veteran's face as he saw that the center of his companion's attention was focused on a table with two girls sitting at it. "I see you have other things on your mind too." A spark of mischief ignited in his eyes. "Hm, is it the lassie with the short, dark hair? What is it with you American chaps and skinny women? She doesn't have enough ballast on her to hold her down in a stiff breeze. I prefer my women with a little more meat on their bones. When I put my arms around her to give her a hug, if my fingers can touch on the other side, then she's too skinny! Why, I remember this one lassie in Liverpool, she was—"

An American Army officer came walking up to the table and The Colonel stopped in mid-story. "Well, you have company here, lad, so I'll be talking with you later." He got up from the table and turned as he left. "Just remember what I said about your boys."

"Thanks," Avery replied with a small smile.

"There you are."

Avery looked up to see First Lieutenant Jason Peters. Peters was Avery's right-hand man and had come to work for him shortly after he'd arrived in England two years ago. He was a tall, lanky twenty-six-year-old drink of water from Alabama with curly blond hair and deep blue eyes. Jason had a bumbling country boy charm that the English girls found irresistible.

"I've been looking for you, sir," Peters said.

The waitress dropped off his fourth beer, and Avery downed half of it in a single gulp. He set it down and wiped the foam from his lips. In all the time he'd been in England, he still hadn't acquired a taste for English beer. He took another gulp and shook his head. What he wouldn't give right now for a hot dog and a *real* cold beer, like he used to get at the Dodgers games!

Peters sat down and put his hand on his boss's shoulder. "Still beating yourself up, Griff? You did everything you could to make sure things went right. Anna and I couldn't find any mistakes when we reviewed the plan."

"Anna," Avery said letting out a long, heavy sigh like a schoolboy with a crush on his first grade teacher. He looked around the room and his eyes stopped when they reached Anna's table. Anna . . . she was the love of his life, only she didn't know it. Anna Roshinko was a second lieutenant who also worked for Avery doing clerical duties. Over the last few months she had been helping him more and more, planning and assisting with her own French resistance cell.

"Look at her, Jay. She's beautiful, and she's as smart as she is good looking." Anna Roshinko was thirty-one with short, ebony hair that framed her heart-shaped face. She was a petite five-foot two inches tall and had a doll's figure that even the Army uniform couldn't hide. Her eyes had the piercing blue color of a northern glacier. Peters chuckled at his tipsy boss, glad for the distraction that took his mind off Strovinski and the failed mission. Roshinko was not bad looking, Peters thought, but not as beautiful as his boss was professing. Then again, he knew Avery was seeing her through a different set of eyes.

Anna sat at a table with her friend, another clerk from the office. The two of them had been there an hour and had been approached twice by American servicemen and three times by British officers, but had politely turned them away.

"Look," Peters said, "Anna's getting up. Looks like she's getting ready to leave. I think she lives somewhere around here. Why don't you go over and ask if you can walk her home? You know, be the gallant gentleman and all."

"I don't know," Avery hesitated. "She'd probably just say no."

"But she might just say yes."

"You think so?"

"Yup. And besides, this isn't the best part of town, you know. Look, there she goes. You'd better hurry."

Paul grew up in Oregon on the shores of the mighty and mysterious Columbia River, and spent endless hours daydreaming on the beach in front of his house, making up stories about the ships from exotic ports all over the world that steamed up the river – what secret cargo might they be carrying; did they harbor spies who were on dark and exciting missions?

Later in adult life, he moved to another mysterious and provocative city – Las Vegas, just outside the famous Nellis Air Force base. After work he would sit on his porch and watch the fighters take off and land, igniting his imagination with visions of secret missions and rich speculation about what could possibly be hidden at Area 51.

After moving back to his native Pacific Northwest, Paul worked for the Navy and took every opportunity he could to speak with veterans from WWII to the Gulf War, listening to them swap stories and relate the experiences of a lifetime.

So it is this combination of a passionate love of history, a vivid "what if" imagination, and a philosophy of life that boils down to the belief that – *there are few things in life that a bigger hammer won't fix* – that led Paul to become a writer of exciting, fact-based action-thrillers. His greatest joy is leaving his readers wondering where the facts end and the fiction begins.

CPSIA information can be obtained at www.ICGtesting.com
Printed in the USA
BVOW08s2129170214

345197BV00002B/3/P

9 780988 618510